READER,
I MARRIED HIM

READER,
I MARRIED HIM

Michèle Roberts

LITTLE, BROWN

A *Little, Brown* Book

First published in Great Britain in 2004
by Little, Brown

Copyright © Michèle Roberts 2004

A CIP catalogue record for this book
is available from the British Library

ISBN 0 316 72750 4

Typeset in Garamond by M Rules
Printed and bound in Great Britain by
Clays Ltd, St Ives plc

Little, Brown
An imprint of
Time Warner Book Group UK
Brettenham House
Lancaster Place
London WC2E 7EN

www.twbg.co.uk

for Mark

ACKNOWLEDGEMENTS

Thanks to Gillon Aitken and all at Gillon Aitken Associates. Thanks to Lennie Goodings and all at Time Warner Books. Thanks to Giuliana Schiavi for explaining the idea of the *capriccio*, the fantastical city, in Italian art. Padenza in this novel is my version of a *capriccio*. Thanks to Sarah LeFanu and Jenny Newman, and to all my other writer friends too. Thanks to Catherine Byron and her colleagues for their support while I was Visiting Professor at Nottingham Trent University, and thanks to all my current colleagues at the University of East Anglia.

CHAPTER ONE

My mother kept her pistol in the wardrobe in her bedroom, thrust into a stack of folded blouses, on the shelf above the rack of skirts and dresses. She ought to have kept it under her pillow, instantly to hand should she have woken to hear a burglar rummaging downstairs or twisting the knob of her door, but she preferred to maintain a certain distance between herself and weapons, as indeed between herself and violence of all kinds.

My father sometimes went away on business, and he gave her the pistol to reassure himself that she would be safe during his absences. He was a shopkeeper, a practical man. He taught her how to aim and fire the gun, and set up a target, so that she could practise, outside in the little yard, flanked on one side by the coal shed and by the garden shed on the other. Bullets ricocheted and whined between the walls as in cowboy films. Finally Papa pronounced Mama proficient. If a burglar did dare to break in he would find Mama ready for him with the pistol cocked and the safety off.

That was Papa's view of the matter. Mama didn't tell him

she kept the gun in the cupboard, safely out of harm's way, and the ammunition in her glove drawer. Papa went off, reassured, on his trips to source supplies for the delicatessen. His family was protected. Whereas all the neighbours knew it would be a patient burglar who would ever get shot, sitting astride the windowsill waiting for Mama to don her dressing-gown and slippers and rummage in the drawer of the bedside table for the key to unlock the wardrobe door.

My stepmother Maude repeated that story to me, over gin and tonics, two days after my husband Hugh's funeral. Maude had come up to London for his Requiem Mass at St Joseph's, Highgate, and his cremation at Golders Green, and I had then accompanied her back to her sheltered housing flat just off The Broadway in Greenhill. She was never one for condolences, Maude, which she judged a sign of weakness. Instead she tried to be bracing, to divert my mind from my sorrow. Part of her role as my stepmother, she considered, involved talking to me about my mother, whom of course she had known well, and thereby, incidentally, proving to me that she, Maude, had a generous soul and only my best interests at heart: the very apotheosis of stepmothers.

I had to rely on Maude's version of the past because unfortunately my mother had died before recounting much of her family history. My mother gave the impression of haste, being thin and nimble and quick, but in fact she didn't hurry. She and my father took turn and turn around in the shop, and on her afternoons off she could spend hours wrestling apart the stove to clean it properly, or sewing beads onto my blue felt waistcoat for the primary school play, or waiting for jam to boil and set. At night she read novels from the public library. She hated short stories, which finished too soon. She taught me to read, then bought me, volume by volume, the Blackie Children's Classics. She must have thought she had plenty of time before filling me in on her own history. I remembered phrases and sentences of hers rather than whole paragraphs. Sayings she'd got from her own mother. A little bit of what you fancy does you good. That's the ticket. Handsome is as handsome does. My mother might have loved books but she herself was like a notebook with most of its pages torn out. People had used them for scribbling lists, or adding up bills, or to make spills for lighting pipes, or the gas. For me she was a paper Ark. How dared she sink when I could barely swim?

Other sources of stories vanished almost as soon as Mama did. Since her death we had rarely visited our relatives, because Maude said it made Papa so sad to be reminded of times gone by, and in fact Maude herself did not care much for them, because she felt they disapproved of her and judged her unfairly, and so relations cooled. Then my father too died, and being socially inept I did not get back in touch with those lost cousins, uncles and aunts. The only remaining person linking me with my past, except for Maude, was my old friend Leonora, faithful and true, who went on sending me postcards, even after she had entered the convent and might have been thought to have had higher things on her mind.

The telling of tales altered according to Maude's mood. Today, the second day of my visit to Greenhill, she fluttered here and there, to and fro across her sitting-room, bored and restless. I'd thrown out her routine. Freed of my presence she'd have been able to get on with planning new dance frocks or sorting out her photograph albums or cooking for the freezer. Those continental dishes she kept in reserve for bridge evenings: mini quiche lorraines made with white sauce rather than eggs and cream, *pommes dauphinois* layered in skimmed milk. As it was, she felt she had to talk to me, occupy my mind.

– Whatever happened to the permit for that pistol, Dawn, I wonder? Goodness knows where it is now. Or perhaps your father never had one in the first place. Guns used to circulate pretty freely in the old days, you know.

She fidgeted back and forth, gin glass in one hand. She twitched at her bouquet of dried hydrangeas in their cut-crystal vase, the silver cups for ballroom dancing which lined the mantelpiece. She re-positioned the photographs on the lace-covered ledge over the radiator which served as her shrine. Here a statue of Our Lady of Lourdes jostled coloured prints of the Pope and Padre Pio, flanked by photos of dead relatives.

Usually my father held prime place in the middle of this display, looking shyly out from an ornate gilt surround, his crinkly hair Brylcreemed and his uniform collar very stiff.

He held his peaked cap under one arm. The photograph must have been taken during the war, just before he married my mother: he seemed so young. People of his generation referred to time in that way: before the war, during the war, after the war. Maude hid more recent pictures of him in her album; she said they made her too sad. The photograph of my mother, her fair hair pinned up in rolls and swoops, peeped from behind Papa's. In life she had been less retiring. She had turned her head and smiled, taken his arm, walked beside him under the trees in Highgate Woods.

A studio portrait of Hugh currently enjoyed centre position in Maude's arrangement of fond memories. In a while, the holy period of remembrance having been correctly observed, he'd be tactfully moved backwards, a soul emerging from purgatory towards heaven; not quite out of sight and so not totally out of mind either.

– Your father's other weapon of choice, Dawn, Maude continued, arranging herself opposite me in an armchair: was a policeman's truncheon he had got from heaven knows where. Probably some man in a pub.

Papa when young worked as a salesman for a firm making fancy cigarette boxes. These might look like miniature pianos, or old books, or tiny chests of drawers. Their lids lifted up to reveal, hey presto, your neat rows of Players, held in place by an elasticised ribbed ribbon of reddish silk. Every Christmas Papa gave me one of these boxes. Samples that came in handy for holding dolls' clothes. Later, Maude threw them away to discourage me from smoking. Papa travelled to far-flung parts: Leicester, Salford, Durham. He was vigorous, newly demobbed and fond of adventuring, and full of curiosity. He enjoyed selling. In those days everybody smoked. Cigs were a good way of meeting people and making friends. Got a light, mate?

The truncheon had a ridged handle. Its end swelled thick and heavy. You could imagine it coming down crack! on an intruder's head. Mama got pregnant with me a year after the wedding day, and Papa decided to settle down to a different job. He borrowed money and bought the deli, and got hold of the pistol, and the truncheon was put away.

Maude liked to recount how Mama took it out again one afternoon in her seventh month. She began boasting to Maude, who was her best friend and who'd popped in for a chat, about how well she could juggle. My mother was apparently often seized with wild whims while pregnant. This was just one of them. Maude egged her on. She challenged her to a demonstration. Mama juggled with two tins of tomatoes, a packet of macaroni, and the truncheon. After a while, when the truncheon whizzed dangerously close to her ear, Maude stopped her and made them both a cup of tea.

– Heaven knows what damage she might have inflicted with that truncheon, Dawn. Her hormones made her very volatile. She could have had an awful accident.

My husband Hugh, he of the wavy hair and strong white teeth, had not left me any weapons with which to defend myself during his final absence. No symbol of his calm and patient attentiveness on which I might depend, on which I might rely in times of confusion. This struck Maude as sad, and foolish too. Who knew what would become of me? Released from a husband's care, I might go completely haywire. She was keeping an eye on me, I knew, in these early days of widowhood, lest I run amok, under the force of grief, and commit who knew what indiscretions and foolishness.

– I remember, if you don't, that terrible time, she said: I'm not one to flinch, as you know, from calling a stone a stone. I mean a spade a spade.

– But I was only thirteen, I protested.

– I had my duty to do, she replied: and I did it.

Careless of Hugh to have died, Maude thought, without leaving me instructions on how to cope. Maude deplored what she saw as my impracticality, romanticism and dreaminess, my capacity for getting too easily carried away beyond my better judgement. The fact that I had got married so often, she often pointed out, only went to prove it.

– Every woman owes it to herself to get married once, Dawn, but you don't have to make a habit of it.

She was quoting from a book, but I didn't know which one. This struck me as odd, since reading remained my favourite hobby, and I considered myself rather well-read. She was being unfair, in any case. I had supposed my marriage to Hugh would last. Well, we do, don't we? That's what marriage means.

My first husband, Tom, a very different sort of man from Hugh, my third, had known the value of mementoes if not of weapons. He had once given me a piece of fool's gold, shaped like a penis, that he had picked up on a beach in Dorset after an open-air rock concert. He put it on my bedroom mantelpiece, before leaving for Germany, so that I could see it as soon as I woke up. Tom's chestnut hair rippled over his shoulders. He wore flowered shirts, flared hipsters. It wasn't his fault he was so attractive. We married too young. How could I expect him to be faithful? The sixties encouraged sexual freedom. The lump of fool's gold was meant to remind me that although Tom had departed to drive the band around Europe, gigging in a different city every night, he would try to resist the advances of the girls who hung around backstage ready for anything, as many girls in those days were, and are still.

– Such an awkward age to become a widow, my stepmother said to me: you'll never get another man now. Men always go for younger women.

– Papa didn't, I reminded her: you were older than he was when you married him.

– Only several years, Maude said: and men are always younger than women, whatever their ages. They're all children really.

Drinking gin at that hour of the afternoon had made us both slump. She sat up straighter and lifted her chin.

– What I mean is, she said, tipping back her melting ice: I had the style, the looks, to carry it off. I knew how to dress. How to make the most of myself.

She glanced at my unpainted fingernails. I knew my face shone pinkly. How unfair to have had such a pretty mother but not to have inherited her capacity to wield a powder-puff. My hairline felt damp with sweat. My armpits too. Maude liked to keep the thermostat turned well up even in June. I had insisted on opening the window, reaching through net frills, struggling with the curtain cords and the double glazing, as soon as we got in from our stroll in the park. I had taken off the black pashmina I had bought for the funeral and the post-funeral tea and which I had worn ever since, but I still felt smothered, on the boil.

I had phoned Leonora in Italy to check on the advis-ability of a black pashmina at a funeral. Were they still fashionable? Too fashionable? No longer fashionable at all? Before the war, during the war, after the war. Oh Papa, oh Mama.

– Black remains always elegant, *cara*, Leonora said: as I should know.

She screeched with laughter across the Alps.

– We've just completed the restoration of the west wing, she said: we're going to inaugurate our new conference centre in a couple of weeks' time. Why not come out and visit? I'm sure you need a change of scene. You could come on retreat. Be a retreatant. Retreatee? You could come to our *convegno*.

What was a *convegno*? I'd forgotten a lot of my Italian. Papa's family had been Italians, generations back, hence our Catholicism, but he had never talked Italian to me. A lost language that wore out as it passed from father to son, a cherished but useless language, put away temporarily and then forgotten. I'd learned Italian through living briefly in Padenza, in the Veneto, with Cecil, my second husband, an architectural historian, he of the spotted bow ties and tweed waistcoats. Cecil was as unlike Hugh as he could possibly be, as Hugh, similarly, was unlike Tom, and indeed Cecil for that matter. I've always liked variety. Inspired by Cecil, I'd had dim ideas of researching my Italian family background, but they came to nothing. Not enough time. Was a *convegno* the same sort of thing that Cecil had so frequently travelled to attend? I didn't find out because a bell in the background summoned Leonora away from the telephone and she rang off.

Maude's small sitting-room was crammed with her favourite bits of furniture she had brought from our old flat in St John's Grove, which she sold when my father died and she felt like moving. Straight into sheltered accommodation she went, to prepare for her old age. I don't want to be a burden on you, Dawn, she had said. I missed the flat, in which I had grown up. But Cecil and I couldn't have afforded to buy it off Maude. We were living with Cecil's parents in Surrey at the time, to save money, because all our income went on financing Cecil's research. He needed to make frequent trips to Italy to check the measurements of the buildings he was writing about. His lecturer's salary was not sufficient, even though I worked as his secretary in the evenings and he got my services for free.

– But the flat's partly mine, I'd said: it ought to be, anyway. I shouldn't have to buy it from her. It's not fair.

I begged Maude not to sell the deli as well. But, like the flat, it was in her name. My father had thought it best. She could do with it as she chose. The mortgage my father had taken out was paid off. Maude was free to dispose of her property as she saw fit.

– Such a common part of town, darling. Who wants to shop in Upper Holloway?

– Archway, I countered: almost Highgate.

Cecil took Maude's side, for it embarrassed him that his wife served behind a counter despite his being such a scholar. He said we were well rid of the flat, so drearily and inharmoniously designed, and would be equally well rid of the deli too. Then Cecil suddenly died, leaving me with many debts, and Maude relented, and I carried on with the shop. I paid Maude a rent, and myself a small salary out of the proceeds. Papa had saved nothing towards a pension, and so Maude could have been destitute, but now, with my weekly payment coming in, her old age was safely provided for.

– Don't worry about me, darling. You're young. You must get on with your life. I'll be fine.

Hugh had put me to shame. Most Sundays, after giving me a hand with the washing-up, he drove over to see

Maude. Sometimes he accompanied her to Mass. I went infrequently to church, since most of the time I considered myself lapsed. Lapsing reminded me of failed soufflés, sunk in the middle. The trick was to announce them as a version of Italian *budino*. Rarely did I get caught out.

Maude glowed, pink-faced from gin and warmth.

– Ah, this is nice, isn't it? So cosy.

Our two purple fringed-velvet armchairs, pulled close, forced our knees almost to touch. The atmosphere, a gloved hand, clamped itself over your mouth. In here everything was covered up, like a scandal in a thriller, the floor with layers of white sheepskin rugs, the surfaces of chairs and tables with throws, antimacassars, piles of embroidered cushions and chenille cloths, the TV with a shawl. Doyleys lay under the filigree pots clenching begonias and spider-plants. Sharp-cornered occasional tables balanced porcelain harlequins ogling crinolined ladies in poke bonnets. Their china-stiffened net skirts sparkled with brilliants. Dolls; but not for children. Underneath them lurked telephones, bowls of barley sugars, jars of pot-pourri. Presents from Hugh to my stepmother, since I disliked such figurines, having learned aesthetic rigour from Cecil, and refused to have them in our flat. Cecil's lessons had been accompanied by sharp intakes of breath when I made mistakes; pursings of lips. Once, when I came back from Habitat with some patterned table napkins, he had paled and been unable to speak for an entire half hour.

Hugh and I had moved into the former storerooms above the deli. Maude, wanting to help the newlyweds, had decided to charge us only a meagre rent, well below the market rate she said. I spent weeks scraping wallpaper and scrubbing walls, ripping up lino. Starting afresh in life, yet again, I meant to do up my new home in elegant Scandinavian style. Ideas copied from an article in *Homes and Gardens,* inspired by an eighteenth-century palace in Copenhagen. Pale green walls, stripped floors with rag rugs, simple beech tables, distressed white dining-chairs with tie-on white cushions, blue-and-white striped ticking curtains. It could have been lovely but Hugh had different plans. His taste ran towards what he'd known himself as a boy. He wanted a patterned wallpaper, a proper fitted carpet, a three-piece suite you could relax on. In the evenings, after toiling all day as a VAT inspector, he came home tired. Peace and quiet he needed. Newspaper, supper, TV.

– A taxing job, working for Customs and Excise, Dawn, ho ho.

He nailed up pictures on the walls that looked quite like real oil paintings until you got up close. He installed storage units housing TV, sound system, home computer, CD towers. I had to keep my books in the bedroom, where space lacked. Now that he had suddenly died, on a walking holiday in Cornwall, I would be able to re-decorate.

A married woman supposedly queened it in her own house but I had never yet managed that. Once Mama died Maude crowned herself queen of our house and queen of wherever I was living, too. At Hugh's funeral she carried herself like the chief mourner, all attitude and hauteur. Partly the effect derived from her towering hat, a black stovepipe wreathed in crisp black lace, but also from her model-like deportment, gloved hands clasped, feet placed in ballet position and shoulders held well back, chin out and stomach in.

— I may be seventy-two, she liked to say: but I refuse to let myself go.

To see Hugh off she wore, with the tall hat, a sleeveless black shift dress, jet earrings and brooch, black stockings, black patent leather court shoes. The flesh of her neck and arms hung slack and loose, mottled orange with fake tan, but she didn't give a damn. She looked like a rich widow on a cruise, waiting for an adventurer to turn up.

— It's probably just as well you and Hugh never had children, she said now: poor fatherless creatures.

Leonora, by email, had suggested Harvey Nichols for my funeral outfit. No hat, she had instructed me. Definitely no mantilla or veil, she had decreed. I had bought a black crêpe vest bound in black silk, with black lace straps over the shoulders, a black chiffon knee length skirt edged with a sheer black flounce, black fishnets, black stilettos. Maude had shaken her head at me and commented that the black pashmina did indeed cover up all the lumps and bumps.

– And with your lifestyle it would never have worked, she said: that's something to console yourself with, anyway.

– Isn't it time for your ballroom dancing? I said.

I got up and put our empty cut-glass tumblers on the little pink and gold papier-mâché tray, decorated with a decoupage Sacred Heart, I had brought back years ago from Padenza.

– What time is Mr Wilson coming to pick you up?

– Dancing is tomorrow, Maude said: though I'm not sure I'll be in the mood. Poor Hugh. Oh, my poor, poor darling.

She widened her eyes and let them fill with tears. She stared at me through swimming pale blue.

– I can't help crying. You know how tenderhearted and empathetic I am. I feel other people's distress so intensely.

I patted her shoulder.

– You're so brave, I said.

Maude blew her nose. I saw her searching for another story with which to cheer us up.

– Now, Dawn, did I ever tell you how your mother first met your father?

I poured us both more gin and sat down again. These sessions reminded me of listening to the Epistles and the Gospels at Mass, which were read aloud, at the appropriate moment, according to a strictly laid-out sequence. You knew exactly which chapters to expect for each particular stage of the liturgical year. Today we were hearing the Gospel according to Maude, Revised Version, chapters one and two.

My mother, aged twenty-one, answered an advertisement in the newspaper, found a job in London. Selling hats.

– I worked in couture before my marriage, that was how she liked to put it to whoever was listening, Maude said: fashion was a serious business then, you know, pre-war. Not only could she sell hats, she could model them as well. Once I'd taught her how. She had the carriage for it. The profile.

London, through the grimy train window, blurred. Just a few tears. Mama stood on the platform feeling like a piece of lost property. Paper labels gummed to her suitcase, cardboard covered with leather veneer, declared her destination and her home address. The suitcase had held her hand all the way from Kent. It tugged her to London, charged up with eagerness. Once arrived, it felt homesick, and sagged, dragging at her side, and then she worried at the fraying loops of twine binding its bent grip, her anxious fingertips fiddling and plucking. She picked at it while pausing to look about her for the newsstand, where she had been instructed to meet her new employer.

Her stockings were too thick. Her new boots were too small. Or else her feet had swollen. The skin on her left heel began to smart, hot and raw, pressed by stiff leather. Mama limped. She sweated in her grey flannel costume and tweed coat, too hot for this weather but too bulky to pack. Cut down from one of her mother's; nipped in at the waist and the hem turned up.

The suitcase weighed too much. It hurt her arm. She halted and dropped it. She took off her coat, folded it, and laid it on top. Then she stood on one foot at a time and released her boots. She placed them, side by side, on the top of the pile. She peeled off her stockings and threw them down. Then she unbuttoned her jacket, unpinned her hat and cast it onto the ground. At this point my father, who had been admiringly watching her performance, came up and offered her a cigarette. He picked up her abandoned gear, and volunteered to accompany her to the bus-stop. She walked away on his arm, springy and barefoot and unencumbered, into the shimmering blue London dusk.

Maude smiled. She raised her hand and tweaked her bouffant. Orange-red, back-combed then fixed with spray, it reared above the high white dome of her forehead.

– Your mother was very lucky, of course, because your father was such a gentleman. He could have taken advantage of her but he didn't.

He had escorted her to the hat shop in Marchmont Street. Her employer had been held up, and very relieved to see the new girl arrived safe and sound. Maude, who had long ago completed her apprenticeship in the shop and been promoted to assistant, welcomed the country mouse.

– The two of us hit it off straight away. Of course your mother was very raw and I had to put her right about lots of things. She looked up to me like an elder sister.

Two good friends. So when one died he married the other. It was sensible and logical. He knew what he was getting, having known Maude all those years. It was a way of being loyal to Mama, also. Not really marrying outside the family, so to speak.

— Your mother converted to Catholicism, to make things easier, Maude would explain: and so naturally I did too, when my turn came.

By the time Mama's suitcase got to me, handed on by Maude, all the leather veneer had rubbed away to cardboard. In it I kept the truncheon that Papa gave Mama and that she had given me for my ninth birthday so that I could play cops and robbers with my friends in the street, the piece of fool's gold that Tom gave me before he suddenly died, and the pistol that was still in Mama's wardrobe when Maude moved it into my room and had vanity units fitted in its stead. Maude tried hard to be a good stepmother. As well as contributing to my cache of weapons she sewed me robbers' outfits: striped jerseys and masks, skinny black slacks.

— Do you take after your mother? Leonora asked me soon after we first met.

— I don't know, I replied.

Mama had got stopped in her tracks. She was in paradise now, with Papa. She had got him back and she was happy again and safe. Was she really?

Not wanting to question the One True Faith at this difficult period in my life, not wanting to think about sad things like death and loss lest I be tempted to cry in front of Maude, which would upset her, I drew the curtains and switched on the TV ready for the news.

Mama would have liked Leonora, who was big, and wild, and shouted, and laughed loudly. Strange how the most unlikely people end up becoming nuns. Leonora had been a feminist in the seventies. She still had very short hair when I met her in Italy in the early eighties. In those days she worked for a feminist theatre company and wrote plays. I met her through Cecil, who liked her because he supposed she was a lesbian, and lesbians excited him sexually. Leonora was interested in England, a place which she considered truly radical for the times. She had even heard of Greenhill, because of the Maoist group based there who travelled all over Europe to demonstrations. She had seen their banner in Venice: Greenhill International Maoist Group.

– Does every north London suburb have a revolutionary Maoist group? she had demanded.

– Certainly not, I had replied.

CHAPTER TWO

Our Lady of Lourdes, greenly luminous in the half-dark, kept watch over me as I undressed. A stoppered bottle: a fountain sealed up, as the Song of Songs had it; a secret spring. Her head, spikily crowned blue, unscrewed and came off so that you could get at the holy water she contained. She perched, inside her plastic grotto edged with tiny shells, on a plastic rock which hid a clockwork mechanism. When you twisted the little lever at the side the rock played 'Ave Maria'.

I slept in the sitting-room because the spare room overflowed with Maude's ballroom-dancing frocks, hung on free-standing racks fitted with quilted poplin dustcovers. Boxes of satin shoes, dyed to match, stood piled underneath. A folding bed slid out from the hall cupboard for my visits. My mattress, an oblong of grey sponge, padded a light aluminium frame. You had to lower yourself down onto it slowly and carefully, to make sure it didn't tip over. A child-sized put-you-up: my feet stuck out over the end.

The clammy nylon sheets made me too hot. I dozed fitfully. In the morning I woke up tired. Mustn't grumble, I said to myself: mustn't grumble. But the small bathroom, with its window of dimpled glass hung with terylene net frills, its pale pink plastic fixtures and pale turquoise walls, its scent of pine and orange air freshener, cramped me. No bath, because that wasted water. Maude had thrown away the bath plug. The shower dribbled, lukewarm.

After a healthy lunch of cos leaves sprinkled with cottage cheese, I accompanied Maude to church. She wanted to go to confession and then stay for Benediction afterwards. We could have taken the bus, but Maude decided the walk would be good exercise, as it was uphill.

— At your age, darling, she said: it's very hard to lose the weight again once it piles on.

I put on my funeral outfit for church, having nothing else suitable with me. Maude wore her pale blue trouser-suit and a matching angora beret. She looked me up and down before we set out.

— Black is so slimming, isn't it?

She frowned at the see-through flounce skimming my knees.

— Are you sure you wouldn't like me to lend you a petticoat, Dawn?

I draped myself in the pashmina and powdered my nose thickly to try and eliminate the shine. Out into Meadowsweet Gardens we stepped. I slowed my stride to accommodate Maude. Obliged to mince in her very high heels, she hung onto my arm. Our dragging pace meant that we arrived late for Confession, at ten past three. I expected a long queue of penitents, since tomorrow celebrated the Feast of the Ascension, a Holy Day of Obligation, and everybody would want to get spiritually freshened up in readiness for High Mass.

I had learned from my second husband Cecil, the bowtied scholar, the international expert on sixteenth-century methods of measurement, to appreciate Renaissance notions of beauty, based on harmony, balance, proportion and the correct following of classical models. The Doric order came first, with the Ionic above, and above that the Corinthian. Maude's parish church disobeyed these rules and so was ugly. But in any case English Catholics couldn't have proper churches because the Protestants had taken them all, back in the sixteenth century. You could only be a real Catholic on the Continent, where the churches were genuinely old, not fake like this one, and smelled as they should, of dust, mould, incense and polish. The church here in Greenhill, representing the height of 1950s Gothic, had been designed for a huge congregation. If this had ever existed it had dwindled. On Sundays nowadays the slatted beech pews were never more than half full. Yet Greenhill, to my childish mind, had been the epitome of spirituality. We sang about it in Assembly: 'There is a green hill far away / without a city wall / where our dear Lord was crucified / who died to save us all.'

Many of Maude's neighbours had begun moving away in recent years because the blacks and Asians were coming in. Maude, however, a keen supporter of the missions in Africa, had been a friend to black people all her life. The nuns at convent school had instilled the same love in me. Every three pence in the collecting box meant you could move your black paper baby one more step up the ladder which stretched up the poster on the classroom wall towards Jesus. The black bambino moved and stopped thanks to a handy gold drawing-pin stuck through his navel. He wore a white nappy. On the top rung of the ladder stood Our Lord and Saviour with his arms outspread in welcome, a crowd of saints, all white, behind him. Half a crown meant a heathen christened, whitewashed, and you got to name the baby you'd had baptised. Africans, the nuns suggested, even when adults, were like children, really. Africa teemed with babies given unsuitable names by me, drawn from my favourite novels: Fitzwilliam, Molly, Dorothea, Edward, Jane. Now Maude welcomed those black and Asian Catholics who occasionally ventured into her church. And where are you from? she would enquire very kindly. Birmingham, they would reply. Some of those newcomers had terrible chips on their shoulders, she warned me: you had to be so careful. Catholicism was international. We were all brothers, thanks to one Pope ruling over all. But perhaps some of us were more brothers than most.

Digging her fingernails into my forearm, Maude processed towards her favourite station in the front pew, with its no-holds-barred view of the altar. Kneeling here, she could be useful. If an altar-boy absented himself from morning Mass she acted as server herself, rang the little bell at the Offertory and the Consecration, made the responses. She ought to have been Pope, Maude, or Prime Minister, or a general commanding armies, but, notwithstanding her lack of official titles, she wore an invisible badge: most crucial laywoman in the parish. Chairman of all the ladies' committees, leader of the Lenten meditation group, chief supporter of the Missions and the fundraising whist drives, every year she ran the Christmas bazaar, and without her input the flower rota would have been nothing. She drew the line at helping with the cleaning. The Irish women parishioners, the lower ranks, the working classes, were responsible for that. They got on with mopping and scrubbing while Maude discreetly supervised.

Entering the cold, clean spaces under the high vaults made me sleepy. I associated this with the crisis of faith I had always felt, as an adolescent, looming during sermons, when I diverted myself by twiddling the clasp of my patent-leather handbag or flicking through the Westminster Hymnal. If I actually listened to the priest's harangue I broke into fits of coughing. The anomie hung in the air like incense smoke. During my absences from church it hid under a gilt-edged cloud like a cushion with an angel sitting firmly on top of it, then burst out and repossessed me next time I came in. Now boredom clung to my mouth, chilly and deadening, like anaesthetic. Like gas at the dentist's. Where would I rather be? Well, in Italy for a start, with Leonora. I wanted a holiday. And then I had Hugh's last request to consider. I ought to be getting on with doing something about it. I definitely ought to go to Italy.

Suspended from a column to the right of the altar on three gold chains, a red glass jar gave out a flickering light. The red glow of the candle signalled the Real Presence hidden inside the Blessed Sacrament. This central mystery of our Faith, impossible to understand with the intellect, dictated that bread and wine changed into the body and blood of Our Lord. We had God physically with us in our churches, unlike the Protestants who had to make do with his spiritual aspect. That made Catholicism superior to other faiths; more true. So Maude made her reverence to God most gracefully, sinking down onto one knee. Then she got stuck. I hauled her up again and followed her into the front pew.

The church plunged down and covered me, a bowl coming over my spider self, God's huge foot looming to squash me flat. The icy blue walls made me shiver. Curving around the apse, high above the altar, a vast 1960s fresco, Italianate in style, depicted the Church Triumphant: the army of saints. Dressed in brown or black and white habits, hands draped in rosaries or clasped in prayer, these doughty warriors were positioned in stately groups, facing the congregation, on the wide marble steps of a lofty staircase. Balustraded, festooned with garlands of lilies, this rose towards celestial distances. St John the Baptist, looking, beside his colleagues in their religious robes, a bit underdressed in a leopard-skin loincloth, broke off his sacred conversation with a heavily armoured archangel, pointed languidly towards the rosy cloud at the very top of the stairs where heaven waited.

Up and up leaped your eye, through the ranked tiers of confessors, virgins, martyrs and patriarchs, until it reached Father, Son and Holy Ghost enthroned in glory. The Blessed Virgin, blue-sashed, blue-veiled and adoring, completed the Holy Family. Like a divorced father, St Joseph lurked sheepishly to one side. Then your gaze slid away and down again. A sort of ecclesiastical snakes and ladders. The Devil disguised himself as a serpent and along his back sinners went down; saints went up. Each saint clutched an identifying symbol: a charity basket; a staff. That had been another way of missing the sermon: working out which saint was which.

Over breakfast I had not been able to stop yawning.

– Perhaps I'll stay indoors after all this afternoon. Have a nap after lunch.

– You and I have so little in common, darling, Maude replied: except our faith. I find that so extraordinary, and so sad, seeing how much I shared with Hugh, and with your father, come to that.

She gazed at me over the flowered china toast rack stacked with pallid triangles of Nimble.

– Don't let me down, Dawn. Let's go to church together,

like Hugh and I always did. Please come to confession with me. I don't ask you for much. Just this one little thing.

I began to make my examination of conscience. I found it hard to concentrate on my sins because the Girl Guides, taking their turn on the cleaning rota, kept clattering self-importantly up and down the side aisles, dropping tins of Brasso and giggling. Their supervisors were the two young Franciscan nuns from the next-door convent school who acted as Guiders. I'd been introduced to them last winter when they took over the Guide troop from the two single ladies, Captain and Kim, who had run it for forty years.

Nobody mentioned the word lesbian in Maude's hearing. I'd once heard her friend Edmund refer to friends of Dorothy and she had looked very puzzled. One morning, not long ago, she and I had taken over-milky Nescafé and a plate of Garibaldis with the two retired officers in their shared bungalow in Carnation Close, and I'd peeped, on my way to the lav, into their bedroom. Twin beds, pink and blue floral counterpanes with frilled valances and matching cushions, twin china shepherdesses topped with pleated lampshades, a shelf of miniature liqueurs, a single kidney-shaped dressing-table.

Once I'd started at the convent school in Greenhill, Maude insisted that I enrol as a Guide myself. I could stay behind at four o'clock each week and spend the two hours, before Guides began, in self-inflicted detention, getting on with my homework. No question of finding a troop of heathen Guides closer to home: only a Catholic troop would suffice.

– But I'm already an Agnesian and a Child of Mary, I pointed out: won't that do?

– I'm adamant, Dawn. Your character is insufficiently formed. You need to learn more discipline.

Since the forces of Communism, in the shape of the Greenhill International Maoist Group, were prone to breaking out in noisy demonstrations at the least provocation, since the local Baptists, Methodists and Presbyterians were only too keen to take to the streets at weekends with their noisy brass bands and raucous hymn-singing, we Catholics had to show we could fight back. Accordingly we learned to drill, marching in fours with Captain leading us up and down, while Kim on the sidelines kept time on a drum and shouted if we broke step. Then we had to run a mile, up and down the Broadway, in ten minutes. I used to arrive back in Archway exhausted. Strange how I could remember these episodes, as clear as images in a slideshow, yet, after the age of sixteen, when I left school, most of my subsequent life remained blank. Of course, I got married very young. That probably accounted for it.

The two nuns began attacking the statues in the side aisle nearby. These saints, on plinths clustered near the confessional, behind iron racks of votive candles, eyed each other with a chummy air. They leaned towards each other, confidentially, like neighbours gossiping over fences.

– Oh, Saint Anthony's come up beautifully, hummed Sister Brigid: I've just Saint Therese to do and we'll be through.

She whisked her polish-stinking cloth over the little Carmelite's chipped face, armful of pink plaster roses, sandalled feet.

– Sssh, hissed her companion, flapping one hand: can't you see people are trying to pray?

Sister Veronica, cut out on Maudish lines, obviously resented having to go on her knees to dust the underneath of pews and scrape candle-wax off the floor in front of Our Lady of Fatima. Equally obviously she loathed Sister Brigid. You could see it in the set of her thin shoulders under the grey crimplene, the tight expression on her triangular white face. I wondered whether she had been set Sister Brigid by Sister Superior as a test of her humility, like the nun in *The Nun's Story* ordered to fail her exams to prove she wasn't proud. English Veronica, the teaching nun who'd studied at the Catholic teacher-training college at Roehampton, despised badly educated, Irish Brigid, who came from a poor family in the countryside and had probably been put into the convent to get rid of her, Maude had pointed out. Convents used to be full of nuns like that, who disliked the life and each other. Veronica would have the rest of her life here to sort that problem out, learn charity. But I wouldn't. Things had begun to fly free of my control. Alterations of all sorts had come upon me.

Maude returned to her place next to me, dropped to her knees, and nudged me. My turn in the black box of the confessional. Like a mini cathedral complete with pointed arches and window slits. Leonora, when I first knew her, had had one in the hallway of her Padenza flat. She had rescued it from a rubbish dump in the early sixties, that time when the Vatican Council's call to *aggiornamento:* meant new brooms sweeping the churches clean of old furniture, literally as well as metaphorically. She kept her clothes in her confessional, summer wardrobe to the right, winter to the left. The Greenhill Catholics, an embattled island in a sea of Protestantism, could not afford Italian light-heartedness. They had retained their little black houses in which you whispered the secrets of your life, your sins.

I pulled the serge curtain to behind me and knelt down on the hard lip of the prie-dieu in the darkness smelling sourly of dust and sweat.

– Bless me, Father, for I have sinned, I began.

I halted, searching for something it felt possible to say. Like being at a party, initiating conversation with a strange man, trying to find a topic that will mildly interest you both but not frighten him off. No getting over-excited. No asking personal questions or becoming too intimate too quickly or pronouncing over-strong opinions. Women's magazines frothed with such counsel. No magazine I had ever read had offered advice on what to say in confession. At school we had relied on lists of venial sins we could check off: I answered my parents back, I forgot to clean my school shoes, I argued with my teacher, and so on. But adults were supposed to manage without such aids.

– I want to get away from people needing sympathy, I muttered to Father Kenneth through the little grille: you'd assume I was the grief-stricken one, wouldn't you, being the widow, but all his friends miss Hugh so acutely, it's very tiring, cheering them up all the time. My stepmother as well.

– What a devoted son-in-law he was, Daphne, Father Kenneth replied: she hadn't many such to join her in a rubber of bridge or practise the foxtrot with her, God bless his soul.

No way did I feel encouraged to tell Father Kenneth any of my real sins, not the major ones, not the mortal ones that merited hell if not properly forgiven; not with him assuming he knew who I was. The embarrassment of bumping into him soon afterwards, on the way out of church or in the off-licence, was unbearable. First he was supposed to pretend he didn't know you, and then that he did. It was the way he muddled the two together and got them the wrong way round that I couldn't stand. I decided that this was the last time I'd ever go to confession. Technically that meant I wouldn't be able to go to Holy Communion, either. Like those women who used birth control and so were barred from the Sacraments. I'd have to be barred too, even though Hugh, that ardent Catholic, had been firm about forbidding the Pill and sticking to the rhythm method. Just to be on the safe side he had practised coitus interruptus as well. He wanted us to delay starting a family until we had some savings in the bank. How long would we have to wait? I married Hugh quite late in life, when I was thirty-five. Then he died and I discovered I was fifty.

– Many a time when I've visited your dear stepmother to say a decade of the rosary with her, Father Kenneth droned on: there Hugh's been, finding good dance music on the radio or teaching her a new game of patience. I've heard her call down blessings on his head. A saint he was, Doreen, and no mistake.

– Saints can be hard to live with, I replied.

I tried to think of something else to confess. It seemed polite to linger a little, not to dash off immediately. I always got stuck with bores at parties because I didn't want to hurt their feelings by moving on. I sometimes thought that was the reason I'd married Hugh. Not knowing how to escape once we'd been introduced. During the interval of the Greenhill Operatic Society's production of *Der Rosenkavalier* in which both Maude and Mr Wilson had taken important roles. And you had to marry the person you had sex with, if you were a Catholic. You were only supposed to have sex if you were married. It was sad to reflect that if Maude was right about my chances, I'd never have sex again. If only I could treat confession as a party: suggest getting Father Kenneth another glass of wine or offer him a cigarette, then run for it.

– I'm worried I didn't love my husband enough, I said: I feel responsible for his death.

– That's women for you, Dixie, he said: always taking too much upon themselves. Feeling like that, child, is a form of vanity. God's in charge, not you, isn't that the truth? So I suggest you leave it to Him. He's the boss! Three Hail Marys for your penance now, and a good Act of Contrition. And now wait while I give you Absolution.

Confession, the Church taught, cleaned your soul in the same way that the nuns were cleaning the church, leaving you spiritually rinsed and sparkling. I knelt at the newly polished altar rails which smelled of synthetic lavender. Behind me Sister Brigid's sandals slapped down the aisle.

I worried about my character sometimes, as of course you do when you're a Catholic, and today more than ever. I couldn't tell any more what I was really like. My feelings flew about all over the place, jumped this way and that. Sometimes I burst into tears without warning. Sometimes I wanted to stamp on things. Or bite them. Sometimes I laughed too loudly. Sometimes I felt that I had been thrown into a deep pit, and nobody knew, and I feared I would die. Sometimes I wanted to eat five platefuls of spaghetti laden with olive oil, one after the other, stuff myself until I could feel nothing but fullness: no emotions whatsoever.

Perhaps I should embark on a course of tranquillisers as well as a diet.

Or perhaps I should get some counselling? As long as it wasn't like confession, with me being required to tell all to someone who never told anything back. As a widow, without the structure of marriage to show me what to do, I had no idea who I was any more. I couldn't remember what it had felt like, being a widow before. Too long ago. I could be this, or I could be that. With Tom I'd been a hippy who smoked dope, listened to David Bowie, threw the I Ching. With Cecil I'd been an elegant and gracious hostess giving art historical dinner parties. With Hugh I'd been a walker, camper, devotee of folk songs and real ale. But now? Alone, I could be anything.

Too frightening. Perhaps I'd gone mad. Perhaps I ought to see a psychiatrist. Better not let Maude know. I felt faint and odd, chaotic inside, my brain dropped to my belly, noisy and dangerous as a swarm of bees.

During my adolescence I had read Albert Camus and decided to become an existentialist. But it had been too hard to stick to for long. You felt so lonely and alone and life was meaningless and death the end and that was that. It all came down to this earth being a vale of tears. Just like the Catholics in fact. I didn't want to go back to being an existentialist again. Over to you, then, God, I prayed: come on, get on with it, if you do really exist. Prove it. Help me!

The little bell tinkled and we all stood up to sing the opening Benediction hymn. Maude's soprano lifted up towards the rafters. She gave it her all. You could hear her especially clearly because she sang in a different key to everybody else.

Benediction was taken by Father Kenneth, plus a priest I didn't know. First of all I noticed his hands. Long fingers. I liked his calm and definite gestures. He had an attractively battered, lived-in face. Greying curly hair, bushy grey eyebrows, a big nose. He was tall. He couldn't have brought his own vestments with him. The borrowed alb was too short on him, the cope as well. His trouser legs stuck out at the bottom and looked foolish. They reminded me of my feet sticking over the end of the put-you-up bed last night. I wondered what he would look like in bed. Whether he wore pyjamas or not. His black shoes loomed, large, and very well polished. *Tantum ergo*, we sang, with the wheezy organ two beats behind: *sacramentum*. Maude's splendid descant rang across the communion rail, into the sanctuary. Father Kenneth, his hands reverently wrapped in the folds of his cope, lifted up the Monstrance, and we all sank to our knees to adore It.

After Benediction Maude and I lingered in the church porch, waiting for Father Kenneth, who'd vanished into the sacristy to doff his robes and get back into his ordinary black jacket, so that we could give him the *Daily Mail* Maude had been keeping for him, with the racing special. The nuns and the Girl Guides pushed past. The sisters nodded at us but didn't stop to chat. Perhaps they were spoiling for a row, which they'd only be able to have outside in the carpark.

While we waited Maude smoothed her gloves and adjusted her beret and I read a pamphlet on the missions and then studied the notices. A handwritten notice, a blurry photograph of St Peter's pinned to it, advertised the forthcoming parish pilgrimage to Rome. Another one promised a trip, later in the year, to Medjugorje.

The longing to go to Italy rose up in me again. I could easily close the deli for a few days if I wanted to get away. I could go and see Leonora. Yes, I would definitely do that.

The double glass doors giving onto the interior of the church burst open. Father Kenneth shouldered through. The tall priest who had co-officiated at Benediction followed. He wore a badly-cut black polyester jacket. His trousers depressed me. They definitely had to be called slacks. More black polyester, with a crease down the front. Free of the swathing vestments he looked nicely built, not thin and not fat, but, muffled by his new variant of priestly disguise, he remained mysterious.

My stepmother advanced and smiled graciously.

– Hello again, Father Kenneth beamed.

He introduced his companion as Father Michael. Maude bent her head regally.

– And how are you enjoying life in this new parish, Father?

– I'm just visiting, Father Michael said: I'm on secondment from the theological college at Golders Green.

– And then this is Dorothy.

– Dawn, my stepmother said: her name is Dawn.

I shook Father Michael's hand. The nuns at school had constantly warned us never to touch priests, because they had touched the Host and we dirty females must not contaminate their holy hands, but I always forgot, having been brought up by my parents with the continental manners Mama had acquired in the hat shop and Papa remembered from his family, to kiss people I scarcely knew let alone clasp their palms. Father Michael's long fingers, dry and warm, closed round mine.

– I'm just visiting too, I told him: and actually my name is Aurora, though most people find it too much of a mouthful.

– It's a lovely name, Aurora, he said: Saint Aurea, virgin, feast day the eleventh of March. You were named after her, I expect. Though I've an idea you come into Dante and Petrarch too. In an allegorical sense, at any rate.

He cocked his head to one side and studied me.

– In that pashmina you look just like Mary Magdalene, coming to the tomb, in one of Giotto's frescoes.

– Maude is a stalwart of the parish, Father Kenneth said: one of my most faithful parishioners.

Father Michael nodded. His eyelids drooped over eyes of an intense dark blue. Slate blue. Almost indigo. Josephine Tey in *The Franchise Affair* asserted that dark blue eyes indicated a criminal, promiscuous and dishonest personality. Well, that just went to show that novels sometimes got it wrong.

– I see you're interested in our pilgrimage next month, Dymphna, Father Kenneth said: it's not too late to sign up for it, and you could bring your dear mother along with you. I'm getting too old for the organising required and so Father Michael here has kindly volunteered to lead the parishioners in my place. I'm just going to be his assistant. I'm sure we've plenty of room in the coach for both of you, isn't that so, Michael?

– Rome, Maude sighed: Mass in the Vatican. An audience with His Holiness. Oh, I should love to come.

She clasped her hands together and looked at me.

– Darling, what d'you think? The Eternal City!

– I'm not sure I'll be able to get away, I said: but you should definitely go, if you want to.

– Come with us, Dilys, Father Kenneth cried: we'll pray together in the Sistine Chapel and we'll gain wondrous indulgences for Hugh's soul, God rest him.

– I'll come, Maude said: Dawn's never been very good in groups. Though a pilgrimage would do her good. Just the thing she needs.

She nodded her head first at me and then at Father Kenneth.

– She mopes, poor thing. The trouble I have persuading her even to leave the house! She wants bucking up. Life's got to go on, hasn't it? Dawn will find that out sooner or later. She'll discover that we just have to get on with it.

Father Michael looked polite and cool. I glowered at the floor.

– Actually, I said: I'm thinking of going on a retreat.

Sort of. The ones at school had necessitated whole days in silence, frequent sermons by the visiting chaplain, lengthy sessions of reading the *Lives of the Saints*, swoony sentimental vigils in front of the Blessed Sacrament in the dim chapel. Whereas what I had in mind thirty-five years on involved chats with Leonora over shots of grappa, buying a new summer wardrobe, sitting in the convent garden under a grape-hung pergola, and smelling the honeysuckle and roses. Possibly nipping into the convent library to consult Petrarch and Dante and see where they mentioned my name.

We took the bus home. Maude kicked off her high heels and put her feet up on the leather pouffe.

– I'll buy a new mantilla. Did Cherie Blair wear one when she visited the Pope, do you know? I think you have to wear a full-length dress for a Papal audience. Black, of course. Pity one never wears black for ballroom dancing. All my gowns are the wrong colour. But I can add on an extra panel to my black brocade cocktail frock. And I can take a bunch of rosaries for His Holiness to bless. That's my Christmas present problem solved for this year.

Mr Wilson, one of Maude's many admirers, turned up at five to accompany her to their Latin American dance class. They had met at an ecumenical cheese and wine party at St Mark's, the local Anglican church, a neo-Byzantine, neo-medieval basilica on the Venetian model.

Edmund had invited Maude to his lecture, to the Greenhill Antiquarians Society, on ecclesiastical mosaics, and the friendship had gone on from there. Retired, he still taught art history to students of evening classes. He specialised in the late Renaissance in Italy and France. With Hugh dead, and unavailable, Maude would have to rely more on friends like Mr Wilson. I provided little help, not being able to drive. Hugh's Ford Escort sat outside the deli, unused. Sooner or later it would get vandalised, or stolen, and I would be rid of it. Maude did not want to get rid of Mr Wilson. She did not want to marry him, either. Eligible he might be, a bachelor with a good pension, but Maude swore she intended to remain faithful to my father's memory.

– There's no other man in the world for me, she liked to say: as Edmund understands so well.

Once I had suggested to her that Mr Wilson might be gay and so not much of a threat to Papa in his grave.

– I hope Edmund would never use that word to me. Of course, whatever they do in private, that's their business, but they don't have to go mentioning it in public. They don't have to rub our noses in it. And it's so wrong the way they've taken over that word. We can't use it any more because we'll be misunderstood if we do.

Nonetheless she needed someone to act as chauffeur so that she could get to all her meetings and do her socialising. Mr Wilson preferred the Anglican Church to the Catholic one, sadly, but you couldn't have everything. Gay or not, he danced well. He chose his clothes with care. He opened doors and carried parcels. Also he was original. *Distingué*, Maude pronounced. He hated using the telephone and only communicated by letter. He wore his black hair in a fringe. Much of the time, indoors too, he sported a trilby hat.

– Edmund, Maude said: come with me to Rome!

– Not this summer, dear lady, he said: I shall make my annual visit to Florence, Venice and Siena, of course, with my little tour group, but this year, in addition, I'm going to stay somewhere quiet, in a quiet hotel, where I can be quite alone, to do some writing. I have decided it is time I began work on my memoirs.

Maude looked at him speculatively. She was obviously wondering whether she would be in them, and if so whether she ought to spice things up a little. Do or say a few more unforgettable things. In my memoirs I would remember the evening when Hugh and I went with Maude to have supper chez Edmund and he complained because we had got the day wrong. He had been expecting us the night before. When we did not turn up he did not, of course, telephone to check what had happened. He had had to eat all the food by himself. Poached salmon, new potatoes, cucumber salad and strawberry tart. He invited us in, nonetheless, and whisked together another meal. Shepherd's pie followed by plums and custard. He put the bowl of custard on the kitchen windowsill to cool. In the dining room we ploughed through our grey mince. When pudding time came cries of anguish issued from the kitchen. The custard had fallen three storeys into the garden below. Edmund reappeared amongst us in his trilby hat, silent and reproachful, and served us the nude plums.

– Supper's in the fridge, Maude told me: a pot of plain yoghurt and a nice plate of salad all ready and some low-fat dressing in the little Tupperware box in the door. Don't wait for me. You know I never eat anything in the evenings. Anything you eat after five p.m. just piles on the weight.

While she was out I had space to move around and think my own thoughts. I decided to wash my hair. I plugged the plug-hole with the rubber plunger I found under the sink, and managed to run a deep bath. I decided to try a relaxation session such as I had read about in *Cosmopolitan*. Conscientiously I emptied some Radox into the water, lit a candle I had found in a drawer in the kitchen, and lay back. I looked at the mound of my stomach rising up in front of me like the world re-emerging from the waters after the Flood. My weight tended to go up and down. Falling in love made me lose my appetite and get slim. Disappointment made me over-eat and get fat. I wondered whether I would ever lose my appetite again. But when nobody nagged me about it I felt quite tender towards my plumpness. Someone had to feel sorry about my disappointments and that person would be me.

I washed and rinsed my hair, felt myself relaxing very nicely, drifting off into plans for my future as though on a gondola making past the Lido for the open sea. I began wondering about following in Papa's footsteps and travelling a bit, using the trip to Italy to source some exciting new supplies for the deli. I could start a nice little line in *mostarda* and other preserves, discover a better class of olive oil, sniff out those foods about to come into fashion. Last year it had been *cavalo nero*. The year before that, rocket. The year before that, *radicchio rosso*. Shopping in Berwick Street market recently I had heard a mutter about beetroot tops and turnip greens. I really ought to find out whether they were already out of fashion as was quite likely the case. I needed to stay ahead of the game. Customers liked it if you were able to discuss their dinner party menus with them and say: oh, polenta, that's so year before last, and suggest something different, something that so far had never been seen on any other Archway table. I could check out those herby liqueurs people drank in the Veneto. I could start to stock grappa.

I must have fallen asleep, because the doorbell chiming the first line of 'Silent Night' woke me up. The bath water had nearly all ebbed away. I floundered in a cold puddle. Clambering out, I seized my dressing-gown and forced my wet arms into the sleeves. The blue silk folds became patched with damp. I flipped back my wet curls with one hand and hurried into the tiny hall. Maude had returned very early. She must have forgotten her keys.

– I wasn't expecting you so soon, I cried, opening the door.

– Sorry, Father Michael said.

I dripped onto the mat and gaped at him. He did not look particularly surprised by my *déshabillé*, as though he met semi-naked women on doorsteps every day of his life. Well, perhaps he did. He was smiling courteously at me. What nice manners he had. What a gent.

He wore black leather gauntlets sheathing his arms, carried a helmet tucked under one elbow. A large motorbike, a Harley Davidson it looked like, reared behind him on the driveway. My first husband, Tom, had ridden a Harley Davidson. I'd always thought them beautiful bikes.

– My stepmother's not here, I said: she won't be back until nine or thereabouts. Can I take a message for her?

He bent forwards. I caught a waft of Eau Sauvage aftershave.

– Actually, it was you I came to see, Aurora, he said: you've been widowed recently, I understand. So I thought I should come round. It's my duty as a priest to offer you support during this troubling time.

I'd been brought up not to argue and certainly not to argue with priests. I stepped back and he followed me into the hall and thence into the sitting-room.

– It's one of the Corporal Works of Mercy, isn't it? I said: visiting the widowed and the sick. Though I can't remember which one. Do sit down. What would you like to drink?

My clothes were scattered about where I'd dropped

them earlier. I kicked my bra and knickers under one of the armchairs while he pretended not to notice and seated himself in the other one. On the same principle as always wearing good underwear in case you get knocked down by a bus, I felt glad I'd been wearing my new ensemble on the day a priest came to call. Black lace, Fenwicks' best, bought specially for the funeral.

I wrestled with the drinks cabinet, concealed inside a ship's wheel set on a wooden column. To unlock the little door at the front and get at the booze you had to steer to port, then do a quick flip to starboard.

– Sherry? I asked: or gin and tonic? Father Kenneth usually has whisky I think.

– He's a bit of a stereotype, isn't he? Father Michael said: gin will be fine.

– I've come to the conclusion, I said: that he does it as a defence. It's an act. All put on. It gives him some privacy inside himself. It must be so hard being a parish priest. People never leave you alone. They're always wanting something.

I cracked open the tonic and fished for ice in the tiny fridge compartment at the base of the column.

– It's hard being a priest full stop, Father Michael said: people don't treat you as a real person. They're always expecting you to behave in some inhuman kind of a way. As though you don't have feelings just like they do.

– Do you have doubts, for example? I asked: I certainly do.

– Doubts are the other side of faith, he said: Saint Thomas Aquinas has plenty to say about that. There's certainly always some aspect of the faith I'm struggling with, that I can't believe. At the moment I seriously doubt the Second Coming. I can't take it literally any more. I have begun searching for a more metaphorical explanation.

I splashed gin into our glasses, added tonic, lemon and ice, and gave one to him. He took a long pull. I sat down opposite him.

– I think women's liberation is the true Second Coming of Christ, don't you, Aurora? I think that's already foreseen in Clement of Alexandria, as a matter of fact. In a manner of speaking. You remember when he takes on the Gnostics and their scorn for created matter? Though one could argue he is, at the same time, ambivalent about that particular heresy.

– My goodness, I exclaimed: you sound just like my best friend. She's a nun in Italy and a terrific feminist.

– What Order is she in? he asked.

– I can't remember, I said: it never seems to matter, I know she's the Abbess and runs everything, she just sort of gets on with it.

I felt stupid and flustered. I pulled my dressing-gown more tightly around my calves. He seemed so clever and intellectual. Talking to him unnerved me, particularly as our knees were almost touching. I'd already seen he was the kind of priest who had Butler's *Lives of the Saints* off pat, and now it seemed clear he had all the philosophical changes of mind of the Fathers of the Church at his fingertips as well. Lovely fingernails he had, too. Almost manicured, they looked. Extremely clean and just the right length. I tore my gaze away from his hands and stared at his feet instead. He was sitting with his legs crossed. The legs of his horrible slacks had ridden up slightly and I could see his socks. Fine cashmere chequered in two shades of blue. Aha: hope for him after all. I like men who care about their socks. It shows they're not conventional. I knew the real reason I was feeling shy was because I found him attractive, despite his polyester costume, and I shouldn't have. But after our second gin I calmed down and began enjoying the conversation.

He expounded to me his views on the cheap sherry commonly used at Mass. Now that the entire congregation, and no longer only the priest, was possibly about to be allowed to take Communion under both kinds, some thought had to be given to buying decent wine.

– The stuff we have to consecrate with is vile, he said: you wouldn't believe. One of the things I'm going to do while we're in Italy is take some time off after the pilgrimage to travel around Umbria and check out the local vineyards. I'm going to go up north too. I've got to go to a conference in the Veneto and give a talk, anyway. I'd like to sample some of those northern wines. It's only right we should have really good wine in church. The Lord's feast requires no less, don't you agree, Aurora?

I loved the way he said my name. The very way he

said you. This was a real I-thou conversation we were having. I felt like Dorothea in *Middlemarch*, when, after her dreary courtship by Casaubon, Will Ladislaw suddenly comes into her life, and they begin the first of those marvellous, tentative discussions that recur throughout the novel, being utterly sincere with each other in a way that the women's magazines of my youth did not believe was possible. But then the young men of my youth had not wanted to talk to us in any case. Only to fuck us. Surely you could both fuck and talk? None of my husbands had thought so, as far as I could recall. It would be interesting to find out if men had changed. But of course, I reminded myself, my sex life was finished. Over. Celibacy, calm and white and quiet, stretched ahead like a convent dormitory full of narrow beds. No more desire and so no more turmoil. Peace perfect peace.

We drained the bottle of gin. I had reached that admirable stage of drunkenness, elated but not yet incoherent.

– You're such a good listener, Aurora, Father Michael said: I feel I can really talk to you. I feel I could tell you anything. I'm such an introvert. I live so much inside myself. It's wonderful to be able to tell somebody what I'm thinking about. You're an extrovert, of course, I can see. Have you read Jung on introversion?

Being a good listener to Father Michael made me feel capable, even powerful. Perhaps that was how priests felt in the confessional. Here was I, dressed appropriately in long robes, being confessed to. I started laughing.

– It's a female sacrament, I said, with a hiccup: chatting. My mother did it through coffee mornings. Then feminists banned those. Consciousness-raising, my friend Leonora calls it.

– Not Sister Leonora Mason of the Brigandines at Padenza? Father Michael asked.

He pronounced her surname in the English way. It sounded strange.

– Actually, I said: you pronounce Mason as though it's spelt with a z. As though it were Mazon. Excuse my mentioning it.

– She's the one organising the conference on the Annunciation and the Visitation I'm going to be speaking at, Father Michael said: how astonishing. What a coincidence. Sorry. I shouldn't use the word coincidence. I mean what a perfect example of synchronicity, as Jung would say.

– She did mention something about a conference on the phone, I said: a *convegno*, she called it. Fancy you knowing Leonora!

My Italian was shamefully rusty. I would have to brush it up. I'd learned to speak it out of sheer need. I had to go to the market and buy something to eat and so I had learned the necessary words. Then when Cecil had been so often away, measuring monuments the length and breadth of Italy, I had needed to be able to talk to the Italian women I had made friends with. To Leonora.

– There's a fabulous Bellini in the church of Santa Croce in Padenza, Father Michael said: I've just realised that's who you remind me of, Aurora. With your big blue eyes, your wide-eyed, innocent gaze, and your long blonde curls tumbling over your shoulders, you're just like one of those three holy women attending on the baptism of Jesus. You're the one holding the bath towel. Or it could be the pashmina.

He decided not to wait and say hello to Maude. His pastoral duty completed, he donned his gloves and helmet, revved his bike, and sped off. I decided that when I got home I would look up Bellini in the public library. I longed for my shop, spice-scented, dark and cool after the jangle and heat of Maude's flat. I would anticipate the pleasures of Italy. I would choose a picnic for myself, open tins and packets. Prosciutto, artichokes in olive oil, Fontina cheese. One of the pleasures of running a deli was being able to pick out something nice to eat at a moment's notice. One of the pleasures of being a widow was going to be eating only when I felt hungry. Meals would no longer have to be regular. Once I got home I'd be able to have lunch in the shop. I would ease off my shoes and sit behind the counter in my basket chair and put my feet up on a stool, drink as many glasses of white wine as I wanted, smoke cigarettes, and read a novel. Perhaps it was time to re-read Penelope Fitzgerald's *Innocence*.

Soon I might be having lunch with Leonora. Something fresh and delicious, whipped up while she talked to me and smoked at the same time. She had taught me to cook when I first met her in Padenza. Cecil had bumped into her in the archive, where she was researching the life of a seventeenth-century laundress. Normally laundresses did not get into history, but there had been some scandal attached to this one and so she made it into the records as having been investigated by the powers that be for some criminal act or other. Cecil, thrilled to have landed a feminist, a possible dyke, brought his catch home so that he could flirt with her in front of me.

That day for our antipasto I served red peppers fried in olive oil with chili; a bit too soft. I hadn't used a high enough heat, been quick enough, shaken the pan enough. The peppers weren't caramelised, blackened at the edges, as they should have been. Cecil pouted. Like Dr Grant in *Mansfield Park*, he insisted on a high standard of home cooking. But Leonora didn't care. She came into the kitchen, sat down and talked to me and laughed her deep laugh. Her lustrous black hair flopped round her face and stuck up on top. She had big black eyes that sparkled, plump rosy lips. Two days later she accompanied us to the New Year's Eve dinner given by the rich art collector whose villa Cecil was currently measuring. She arrived all dressed up: sleeveless black polo neck, short black skirt, black lace stockings. She sported little bronze roses on the toes of her pumps, glittery gel on her bare shoulders.

Cecil and I both fell in love with her. I think he wanted to go to bed with us and see what dykes got up to but Leonora showed no interest.

– Oh, *cara*, she said with a bellow of laughter: I think he should stick to his researches in the archive, don't you?

I remember her walking around the villa that night, examining its doorways and windows, its staircases and corridors, for all the world as though she had been a proper architectural student.

– I'd like to have a house like this, she informed me: and I will too, one day. You just wait and see.

Shortly afterwards Cecil died, I moved back to England, and we lost touch. She vanished. Via Cecil's former colleagues, when I bumped into them by accident, I occasionally heard rumours: that she was running a sex club, that she had adopted a child, that she was working with prostitutes, that she was writing a book about the seventeenth-century laundress, that she had become a property speculator. When she surfaced and got back in touch with me she was unapologetic. Oh, she said: I've been sorting things out. She had become a nun. Joined the Brigandines and been swiftly promoted to Abbess.

Modern nuns could enjoy holidays and receive their friends. I hadn't taken advantage of these relaxed rules. Though we talked on the telephone and wrote letters, I hadn't seen Leonora for many years. As though I'd been the enclosed one. Our lack of visits hadn't mattered for a long time. But now, suddenly, it did. I had an urgent need to get away and there was nowhere I would rather go than to see my Italian friend.

I flipped through the pages of my address book. L for Leonora. I picked up Maude's phone and rang the Brigandine convent.

– I'm thinking of coming to Italy, I said: can I come and visit you?

– Certainly, *tesoro*, Leonora said: about time too, don't you think?

– What can I bring you? Lemon curd? A jar of mince-meat? You still like malt whisky, don't you? Oatcakes? Marmite?

– Don't be disgusting, *cara*, Leonora said.

I could hear her shuddering. There was a pause, the scrape of a match, the intake of breath. So she still smoked.

– Actually, *tesoro*, there is something that I'm in need of, Leonora said: there's something you could lend me if you've still got it.

Chapter Three

My visit to Maude was at an end. In two days' time she would be off to Rome.

– Help me tidy my jewellery box, Dawn, before you go.

She escorted me into her bedroom. Dominated by an eighteenth-century-style fourposter hung with white satin, lined with fitted cupboards, carpeted in pale apricot, it held several gilt-framed reproductions of paintings of girls by Renoir and one large photograph of the Pope. Maude poked about in her pink and silver jewel casket lined with blue velvet.

– You've seen all these before, darling, haven't you?

She showed me the gold ear-studs and bangle that my father had given Mama as Christmas presents, and that Maude had inherited since I was too young for them, the string of pearls with a pearl added each birthday, the diamond engagement ring, the diamond eternity ring. She held them up, one by one, and stroked them.

– They are beautiful, I agreed: I've got nothing half as nice. I've never kept a husband long enough to be in receipt of such jewels.

I hadn't had the jewel-giving sort of husband. Tom and I had married with a curtain ring, as a bit of a joke. He had not wanted conventional wedding rings: bourgeois marks of possession. Cecil rejected them because they were lacking in taste. Jewellery in general was vulgar. Any spare money went on first editions of great architectural works. I had married Hugh using the curtain ring again. That seemed to be that.

– Try not to be bitter, darling, Maude said: and in any case you're wrong. How about that lovely silver Miraculous Medal that Hugh gave you when you got engaged?

I folded up the aluminium bed for the last time and stowed it away in the hall cupboard. Maude searched around for a farewell present. She pressed upon me a pocket diary that had arrived free from Cancer Research.

– I know it's June. But I'm sure some of those phone numbers will come in handy. And the tube map.

Back in my flat above the deli in Labyrinth Street I made simple preparations for my holiday. I emptied the deep freeze and the chill cabinet and put the contents on sale, so that no perishable goods would be left behind to go off. The buffalo mozzarella, the Milanese salami, the bouquets of sage and rocket and marjoram: I flogged the lot at bargain prices. A notice on the door informed my faithful customers of my five days' closure. Another notice, prominently displayed, signalled the presence of an efficient burglar alarm. Then, nine days after leaving Maude,

I locked up and jumped on the number 24 bus, en route for Victoria and Gatwick Airport.

– Oh, *cara*, Leonora had cried down the phone: why didn't you tell me sooner you were definitely going to come? I'd have reserved you a room for the whole week.

– No, just five days, I said: in fact I'm looking at it as a long weekend.

– As it is, Leonora went on: at the moment we're completely booked up with retreatants, and then after that all the delegates for the *convegno* will be staying because it's so convenient and we do a special rate. I can put you up on the night you arrive but no more.

– That will be fine, I said: I'll find somewhere in town, don't worry. I'll try that cheap hotel in Contra S. Stefano, what's it called, the Tre Marie.

Flying over the jagged teeth of the Alps I swigged gin and tonic, celebrating my departure for that land which so many English people, if their novels were anything to go by, saw as paradise, a return to the Golden Age, a fairytale locus, a mythical site offering personal transformation, rapture, and radical change, let alone excellent shopping in the shape of well-cut clothes and stylish leather handbags.

I had chosen to leave for Italy on a Wednesday, the very day that the parish pilgrims were due to return home. It struck me that perhaps I was escaping something. Escaping what? I didn't want to think about it. Maude had brought me up to examine my conscience in preparation for confession, but not to ponder my motives, considering an interest in psychology a sign of self-indulgence liable to lead to mental instability and subsequent madness. I ordered another gin instead and waved in my head to Maude, Father Kenneth and the parishioners, all jetting back the other way, perhaps crossing our path at this very moment behind a veil of cloud, blissed out, blessed and beatific after seeing the Pope and the major basilicas and the very spot whence the Beatification of Padre Pio had been announced.

We touched down at Treviso airport. Not long afterwards I was sitting with Leonora in my large wooden bed in the guesthouse of her convent. We sipped camomile tea, brewed from camomile grown in the nuns' kitchen garden, from large pale green porcelain cups. I wasn't keen on herbal infusions, but the earliness of the hour forbade cocktails. Leonora had come to join me once I woke up from the siesta she had insisted I must need after my journey. She pulled off her wimple and veil and cast them onto the floor. The bed was so high that there was a little wooden step placed next to it. Leonora clambered up this and arranged herself next to me. She leaned back against the fat pillows I had heaped up behind her, against the antique headboard, and settled her cup and saucer into a dent in the covers.

– Bed's one of my favourite places for a conversation, she said: I like being tucked up in a cocoon with a friend. Have you got enough quilt?

I had slept well in this restful place, the chapel bells chiming through my unruly dreams, in which, clad only in my new French knickers, a confection of black lace which had a side fastening, I capered through the streets of Greenhill. Father Michael, naked, his brown torso spiralled with grey hair, opened the door of a restaurant and beckoned me in. Gazing into my eyes, he peeled my knickers off.

Waking slowly and pleasurably, I contemplated the whitewashed walls of the guestroom, its red-tiled floor, the bronze can of blue hydrangeas under the muslin-frilled window. Holy poverty might mean simplicity for the nuns but translated into luxury, even opulence, offered to visitors. The mattress on the wide bed was thick and soft, the white linen pillowcases and sheets were lace-edged, the embroidered coverlet fat and silky. A walnut side-table held a bottle of wine, a stoppered decanter of water, two wineglasses, a pile of books of poetry. A small cupboard, smelling faintly of lavender and mothballs, bulged with extra quilts.

A curtained archway led to the bathroom, tucked away in what Leonora said had formerly been an oratory. This little temple of chrome, enamel and large dark blue tiles was furnished with stacks of hand towels, face towels and bath towels, a row of glass bottles of bath salts and body lotions, a basket of herbal soaps. All these unguents, Leonora had explained, were made by the convent apothecary using essential oils extracted from plants grown in the garden outside. Sister Clara prescribed perfumes to her sisters on the aromatherapy principle. Tried and tested by the nuns, the oils and scents could then be offered to the convent's visitors, and sold in the convent shop.

Leonora, when she embraced me on my arrival, smelled of rose geranium and lemon verbena. She had brought me, on the tea-tray, a flask of rosemary shampoo. Her own hair, once free of coif and veil, smelled, as she lay back next to me, of strawberries. Her big black eyes gleamed as she explained all the new developments.

– If the convent's to continue being self-sufficient we've got to move with the times, or we'll go under. Modern pilgrims are hypocrites really. They want all the comforts of an hotel, but they like it to come in an antique casing. That way they can have the best of both worlds.

– Pilgrims? I said.

– Ah, I haven't told you yet, she said in her contralto voice: I'll show you after supper.

I'd missed the guttural and deep accents of the voices of Italian women. Their hoarse music. Outside I could hear two of the nuns laughing in the courtyard. I guessed they were winding up buckets of water from the well. Creak, creak, went the handle of the well. Thunk, thunk, went the buckets onto the paving-stones. A cock crowed. Pigeons burped and cooed. I'd pulled the shutters to before getting into bed, and now their inner edges were outlined in warm gold.

The dimness of the room smoothed away wrinkles and lines. Leonora looked exactly as she had twenty years before. She turned her strong profile towards me, her short hair sticking up in all directions.

– And you got through customs all right carrying your contraband? Well, I suppose you must have been looking extremely respectable in that black suit.

The suit lay, neatly folded, over the back of a curly-legged chair.

– It's really rather terrible isn't it, *tesoro*, that outfit, said Leonora: it depresses me to look at it. Why don't we throw it away?

– Fine, I said: I was thinking of buying some new clothes anyway.

– I know everybody in London loves wearing black but here you don't need to, Leonora said: we in Italy like colours. Only nuns and widows wear black.

– I am a widow, I said.

– There's black and black, Leonora said: yours is the wrong kind. I must say that handbag is not very nice either.

I like to travel light. My bulky handbag formed my only item of luggage. Arriving at the airport I carried it very carefully in my arms. No trouble at check-in. I made towards Departures, showed my passport and boarding card, queued for the X-ray machine. I set the handbag down on the moving belt, propping it so that it could not topple over, watched it disappear, then walked through the metal detector arch to collect it on the other side. Before I could rescue it, however, a hand reached out in front of me and lifted the bag aside. Smack! Down it went onto a table. I started forwards.

– Oh, please don't knock it about. The contents are rather fragile.

The little eyes of the maroon-uniformed officer gleamed with suspicion. He stroked his caterpillar-like moustache.

– Open your bag, please, madam. Looks like you've got some dodgy contents there.

I opened it. Wallet, passport, airline ticket, clean white handkerchief, mobile, box of sanitary towels, blue silk dressing-gown, paperback copy of *Middlemarch*, makeup bag, toothbrush and toothpaste, notebook, pen, purse, keys, change of underwear.

– What's this? What's inside here?

He prodded my box of sanitary towels.

– Just my dildo, I explained: I never travel anywhere without it. I'm on my own, you see.

He smirked, and prodded again.

– And what's this? More sexual aids? Thank heavens my wife's never needed them.

A metal canister with a screw top, spray-painted gold. I had a whole row of these canisters at the deli. Formerly stuffed with *amaretti*, subsequently they came in immensely useful for storing all kinds of things.

– Taking your own teabags with you, are you? No, I do

believe it's a cocktail shaker. Open it for me, madam, would you, please?

I sighed.

– I really don't want to have to do this. It seems disrespectful. Nonetheless. If you insist.

I unscrewed the round lid of the canister. The official looked at the white powder inside. Then at me, at my . black trouser suit.

– Don't tell me. You're a widow and these are your husband's ashes and for some reason you can't travel without them, either.

– Got it in one, I said: he requested that they should be scattered in some particularly beautiful spot. He didn't specify which. So I decided on Italy. I am simply carrying out his final wishes.

– And I'm Santa Claus, said the official.

He grasped his maroon lapels and frowned. Then he smiled at me. His little eyes vanished in creases of flesh.

– Only joking. Going to scatter the old man's ashes in Italy, eh? That's so touching. That's so sweet. I went to the Blue Grotto on the Isle of Capri on my honeymoon. Ever been there? That's a nice place. You might consider it.

He waved.

– All right. On your way. Careful with that sex contraption, eh?

Leonora set down her empty cup, sat up expectantly and folded her hands into the sleeves of her habit. I hopped out of bed and seized my handbag.

– Shall I give it to you now?

– Thanks, *cara*. If you would.

I opened the box of sanitary towels, eased out a couple, and extracted the pistol from its snug nest underneath, wadded in soft cotton. Leonora took it from me in the same way Father Kenneth had held the Monstrance at Benediction, reverently, her hands covered by her loose cuffs.

– No fingerprints, eh? I joked.

She twisted to one side under the quilt and slid the pistol into the deep pocket concealed by her scapular.

– Thank you, *tesoro*, so much. And the bullets?

I extracted them and handed them over.

– Here you are.

The chapel bell began to ring urgently. One single, repeated note. Clang, clang, clang.

Leonora kissed my cheek.

– Time for spiritual reading. I must be off. We're just finishing taking another look at *Das Kapital*. Father Michael recommended it last week, when he phoned up to discuss his paper for the *convegno*. Some of the jokes are really quite good.

She got up, donned her coif and pinned on her veil.

– Have a nice walk. I'll see you later for supper.

The community was housed in a villa built in the early seventeenth century on the site of a much older, half-ruined house. The particular spot had originally been chosen, Leonora had explained, because it possessed a good source of water. As often happened, the well built over the spring had become associated with magic and miracles. First a fertility goddess, Brigga, was venerated there, and later a medieval saint, Briganda, credited with helping the local women get pregnant. The cult fell into disuse around the era of the Counter-Reformation, which was also the time when the rich woman who owned the property had it restored in contemporary fashion. Founding her new Order, she gave the nuns Briganda as their patroness.

Upon arrival I had looked at the villa-turned-convent from Cecil's perspective. I'd never laid eyes on it before, when I had lived briefly in Padenza with Cecil, because it was clean out of Cecil's period and so, he had explained, not worth visiting. All my previous sightseeing in Padenza had been done in the heart of town, which was crammed with sixteenth-century buildings, enough to keep Cecil measuring for several lifetimes.

Post-Balladian, designed by an admirer and rival of Balladio, the famous son of Padenza who had revolu-tionised post-Renaissance architecture right across the Veneto, the convent was built in classical style but with more decoration than the maestro would have approved as proper. The portico lacked a relationship of perfect pro-portion to the façade as a whole, and the capitals gracing the Corinthian columns holding up the portico were probably, to the expert eye, over-ornate. A little out of control. More like the feathery tops of celery than neatly curled acanthus. But the villa's very imperfections, Leonora said, were why the Foundress had been happy to give it away and plant nuns in it.

Once this lady had become a widow she had decided she needed a change and had moved out. She had gone off and restored a smaller house on a hill on the opposite side of the city, converting it into a comfortable villa, using a different though still neo-Balladian architect. She did not want to be a nun herself. She installed as novices all the girls of her family who could not get husbands, and visited them frequently. Despite the local prelates' struggles to have the nuns completely enclosed, all the doors, except one, and most of the windows, bricked up, and all visitors forbidden, the Foundress managed to wriggle around the harsh rules. She donated money to the Bishop's charitable enterprises in exchange for his turning a blind eye to what went on up at the convent. Innocent activities: a little lute-playing here, a little acting of masques there, impromptu poetry readings in the garden, organ recitals of the newest music in the chapel. The convent became famous over the years, in a discreet sort of a way, for its hospitality, a tradition that Leonora continued.

Generations of Abbesses had subsequently improved the villa, further adapting it for conventual use. The wings on either side of the main house, formerly stable blocks and barns, were now converted to chapel and guesthouse. A cloister had been built by enclosing, on its fourth, open side, the colonnaded yard at the back which gave onto the vine-planted *brolo*. The kitchen and cellars hid in the semi-basement underneath the flight of steps up to the entrance. Cypresses had been grown along the driveway which led to the house from the gate in the surrounding high wall. A neat terrace flanked the building to the south; a walled meadow and formal garden stretched to one side. Beyond these: the orangery, farm buildings and farmlands. Under Leonora's management the statues of gods and goddesses decorating the terrace, which had been removed by a former Abbess and stored in the attic, were put back, the frescoes of nymphs and satyrs in the main rooms restored, the cellar once more stocked with wine from the now-flourishing vineyard. The nuns baked their own bread, made medicines, cobbled their own shoes.

– I can't remember, did you ever tell me, do you run a car? I had asked over the telephone: I thought the convent was inaccessible by road?

– Of course we do, *cara*. We're not enclosed. We can go out if we want to. We keep the car down in the town, in the Museum carpark. God travels with us wherever we go. He's in the car just as much as in the chapel. Just as well, considering how fast some of the sisters drive.

Dressed once more in my dreary black trouser-suit, I descended the marble staircase that connected the convent to the town below. It hugged the hill on one side, and was arcaded on the other, zigzagging down the steep slope under loops of climbing roses and wisteria. The radiant blue sky was scissored by swifts. Below me the compact little city of Padenza lifted its towers and spires, a rock in a green sea of maize fields. I plunged into it as though falling from the clouds.

The huge Renaissance basilica dominated the Piazza to the west. Rows of palaces lined the other three sides. Twin columns crowned with lions, on the Venetian model, reared up at one end, a statue of Balladio at the other.

Padentines strolled to and fro. I had forgotten the bravura of the late-afternoon parade, how much the Padentines adored clothes. Well, theirs was a city famed for its textiles, after all, and they were out to demonstrate the skill of the city's tailors. What costumes! A girl in a green tunic with red ankle boots. A plump teenager in white cotton skirt and top embroidered in pale pink flowers, sashed with pale pink ribbon, a string of yellow beads around her neck and a yellow silk rose in her hair. She twirled for her group of friends so that they could admire her. Boys in long shorts. A fat woman in a twenties flowered chiffon frock belted at the hips swayed along pulling two toddlers in silk dungarees. Smart babies, attired in knickerbockers and matching satin sandals, lolled regally in their perambulators, waving gracefully, like Jesus in his crib. Just one or two little girls were running and jumping; most walked stiffly as mechanical dolls in their starched ruffles. They were watched by a band of heavily painted matrons, ruthlessly coiffed. Some wore short-sleeved jackets with shoulder-pads, very short skirts, spindly heels. Others sported glittering metallic sweaters, embroidered with sequins and diamanté appliqué, over tight white jeans and flower-adorned high-heeled sandals. By comparison, the tourists, in their shorts and trainers, looked underdressed as well as sweaty and hot. I felt under-dressed too, and dowdy, wearing the trousers of my black suit and carrying the jacket slung over one arm.

I walked around the corner into Corso Balladio to buy a newspaper and check out the shop windows. Plenty of delicious clothes in the shops here. I would come back later. The *passegiata* was more important. I retraced my steps. Passing the side entrance of the Gran' Caffe SS Pietro e Paulo, I decided I'd stop for an *aperitivo*. A white wine spritzer, perhaps, or a glass of prosecco. I walked through the *caffe* and out onto the terrace, set with urns of white daisies and shaded by white parasols. I chose a table at its far end so that I could look out onto the Piazza, separated from it only by a row of bay trees in white-painted tubs.

A couple of fair-haired English ladies, wearing navy blazers over flowery frocks, panama hats and cream-coloured slingbacks, occupied the table next to mine. Sitting with his back to me, a man wearing a bright blue suit and a trilby hat was addressing them as they sipped at their tall glasses of what looked like iced coffee. He spoke as though he had a mouth full of marbles. There was something familiar about his enunciation.

– Lovely to have made your acquaintance, dear ladies, and to enjoy the refreshment afforded by feminine company. Before arriving here I was working so hard. Of course my students deserve only the very best. But this year I have decided I must nourish my own soul as well as do research for my lectures. So I have escaped here, now that my little tour has ended, for precious time alone.

I gazed towards the airy white bulk of the Basilica opposite. My attention was caught by a passer-by with exquisitely fitting pale khaki combats which clung to his hips, emphasising their neatness and narrowness. Strolling insouciantly along, he reminded me of someone I'd known twenty years ago, someone who used to wear finely tailored trousers, tightly belted at his slender waist and falling down in faultless pleats over his shoes. Now I remembered. Only one person in the world had achieved a drape like that. Frederico Pagan, Deputy Director of the Padentine Municipal Museum, and an erstwhile colleague of my second husband Cecil. As he went by I lifted my hand and tentatively waved. I didn't call to him. I'd been brought up not to make a noise in public.

Frederico frowned and looked faintly puzzled for a moment. His expression became cool and blank. Then, as he recognised me, his lean brown face was transformed to liveliness by a smile. He seemed hardly changed in twenty years. He was still as youthful-looking as when I first met him, making a speech at the drinks party celebrating the restoration of the Museum portico. His dark hair still flopped above almond-shaped brown eyes. He still wore beautiful trousers. I could see everybody in the Gran' Caffe SS Pietro e Paulo covertly admiring them, apart from the man at the next table who was still talking loudly.

– Oh! Oh! Some tourists get in such a flap, not knowing what to do or look at first. But even I am astonished by the very great art in this city. It is wonderful. It is riveting. I adore art, of course, and I try to transmit that adoration to my students. Sometimes, I fear, I am labouring to sow my seed on stony ground.

Frederico bounded through an opening between the pots of bay trees and arrived at my table in a graceful leap. He bowed. He seized my hand and kissed it. I caught a waft of his aftershave. Juniper. The same berry as gin. What a good choice.

– Aurora. I was so sorry to hear of Cecil's death. What a loss to the international community of scholars! And then Hugh too. Leonora told me. What terrible tragedies for you to bear.

I bowed my head.

Beside me the blue-suited man boomed towards his climax.

– You can see a lot of art in London, of course. But I adore Italy. So I have this tremendous feeling that I want to come here as often as I can. I look in the window of the travel agents and I yearn. I yearn.

Edmund. Oh Lord. Why wasn't he in Venice, or Vicenza, or Mantua, or Padua? How dare he be here? It is odd how, despite being English oneself, one hates the other English abroad. One does not wish to be associated with them. One wants to ignore them and deny their existence. Accordingly, I shifted my chair and turned my back on my compatriot and the two companions he'd picked up. How upset Maude would be if she knew Edmund hobnobbed with ladies other than herself.

– Let us have an aperitif, Frederico said: but not here. This is an over-decorated place.

Edmund's voice sank to a murmur. A finishing flourish.

– This year I have begun writing my memoirs. And so I've come here for the solitude, peace and repose that that necessitates. But I should love to join you for dinner tonight. Thank you. Yes, I will make an exception just this once.

I got up, collected my bag. Frederico took my arm and steered me across the Piazza, round the side of the Basilica towards Piazza delle Erbe, into the little extension of the main piazza that was dominated by the statue of Balladio's wife Elizabetta. She, I remembered, had been a celebrated cook. What her husband had designed in stone, she had sculpted in pastry, in choux buns, in non-lapsed soufflés. We sat down outside the bar there, the Caffe Elizabetta, which was also a cake shop. I remembered now that this had always been Frederico's favourite place for a drink. The Gran' Caffe SS Pietro e Paulo was too flashy for him. His taste was all to do with the less obvious. His manners, like his trousers, had always been elegant but withal restrained. For example, though I had known from Cecil that he was gay, I'd never heard any gossip about his love affairs. Unlike other of Cecil's colleagues he had never, apparently, wanted to reveal details of his personal life. Cecil, who liked to suck things out of other people, and collect galleries of secrets and titbits of intimate confessions, had thought Frederico standoffish. Frederico didn't want to talk about himself, he would announce, pouting, after a dinner-party or a meeting. Good for Frederico, I would think.

We sat facing the dark front of the *pasticceria*. The old-fashioned window displayed tarts and pastry twists ravishing in their plainness. None of the mounds of whipped cream, technicolour fruits and over-jellied glazes displayed by inferior establishments. One glass shelf held a single gilt stand heaped with pale yellow conical twirls dusted with fine icing sugar.

– Almond cakes, Frederico said, following my gaze: Leonora's nuns make those. It's one of their new departures, to turn the convent into more of a tourist attraction and bring in some extra money. People don't always want to trek up to the convent to buy them, it's such a hot, steep climb in summer, so the nuns bring them down here and sell them to the shop. They're very good, I must say. Would you like to try one?

– Not at this hour, I said: I'd rather have a cigarette if you've got any.

All three of my husbands had hated me to smoke. I lit up and took a deep drag. We drank Campari and chatted. Frederico told me of developments at the Museum. The former Director having retired, he had been promoted to Director in his place. Eager to effect improvements, he was sorting through the as yet unclassified materials in the basement vaults, clearing space to make room for a restoration workshop.

– And we've got our new textiles gallery opening very soon with a special exhibition, timed to coincide with Leonora's conference. I hope you'll still be here? I'll send you an invitation. Where are you staying?

– I'm not sure, I said: I'm at Leonora's tonight, but after tomorrow she's full. So in a minute I'm going to look for an hotel. I thought I'd try the Tre Marie.

– Oh, you can't stay there, Frederico said: it's not a nice place. The floors are turn-of-the-century chipped marble. They look exactly like salami, of the greasiest sort. Anyway it's probably full up with tourists and art history students. Padenza is packed at the moment, I am afraid.

– Oh, I'll find something, I said: something will turn up.

– That's that man in Dickens, isn't it? Frederico said: Mr Micawber. I love Dickens. I love English novels. Sir Walter Scott also.

– Many Italians do, I've noticed, I said: the first time I came here I thought the city was remarkably full of Scotsmen. Then I realised that it was simply all the local Italian men dressed in fashionable clothes.

– Don't forget the Englishmen trying to look Italian, Frederico said.

Talking to Frederico made me feel I belonged in this city. All around us people sat and chattered, sipping their *aperitivi*. At the edge of the Piazza they stood in groups talking and laughing. Golden light washed the stone columns, the sky changing from luminous blue towards indigo. The Angelus began to ring, a tumbling of bells from all over the city. The signal for the end of the working day, for suppertime. Hunger jabbed me. The food on the flight had been inedible and so I had had no lunch.

– How's your mother? I asked.

I'd met Contessa Pagan just once before. There were an awful lot of counts and countesses in the Veneto, and an awful lot of them hanging around the cultural scene, and Cecil had decided to measure up every one of their villas. Unfortunately he had died before completing his great project. *Architectura longa, vita breva.*

– Oh, she's very well, Frederico answered: why don't you come to dinner with us one evening? She would love to see you again.

– All right, I said: I will.

– Come the day after tomorrow, he said: I'll pick you up after I finish work. We close at seven. Meet me under the Museum portico and I'll drive you out.

He put his cigarettes back into his breast pocket. Then he smote his forehead with one hand.

– But what am I thinking of! Aurora, I have the answer to your problem. I've got a tiny apartment in the Museum, that I've had made on the mezzanine floor, which I use sometimes when I've had to stay late working. You can have that. You are most welcome. Come tomorrow, when you move out of Leonora's. Come at eleven, and I'll show it to you.

We got up. He kissed me on both cheeks.

– Until tomorrow, then.

I tried to thank him. He cut me short.

– For Cecil's widow nothing is too good. I am delighted I can be of service to you.

I walked back up the hill. Three hundred shallow steps of pockmarked pink marble brought me to the wrought-iron gate. I opened it with the key Leonora had given me and wandered slowly up the dusty avenue under the cypresses. I could smell the sweet scent of box released into the blue evening.

I reached the cloister just as the bell began to clang. Unsure where to go next, I waited in the cloister garth: a square garden, divided by narrow gravel paths, edged with low hedges, into four. Each little compartment brimmed with grass and held a single rose tree. At the centre, where the paths met, stood a well. I peered at it. It didn't look particularly sacred. Just like an ordinary Italian well with a wide lip. Terracotta pots of miniature lemon trees, the fruits gleaming between glossy evergreen leaves, clustered near it. The cloister, arching around, supported the storey projecting above, its façade pierced with the little windows of the cells. The cloister columns were Ionic. Not classically perfect. The capitals looked a little too much like sliced sections of mushrooms with curled-over ends to be quite right. The capitals of the doorway to the chapel were carved with grimacing and capering beasts, some with human faces. Not classically correct at all. They must have formed part of the earlier building, I thought, and been incorporated into the later design. How simple that was. Water and stone and greenery: they provided peace and silence and calm.

The calm broke up. Nuns came dashing out of doors on every side. They flapped and hopped like pigeons. The young women in pale blue dresses, with pale blue head-scarves tied behind their heads, must be the postulants, I decided. The nuns in grey with white wimples and veils were clearly the novices. The sisters in black, with black veils like Leonora's, must be the professed. We all nodded and smiled at one another, and they waved me to go ahead of them into the refectory, where Leonora waited for us.

The refectory, cool and dim, a well-proportioned oblong room, had high windows all along one side. Along the facing wall stretched a fresco of The Last Supper.

– Painted by one of our nuns, Leonora said: back in 1630. Not bad.

Beneath it was The Next Supper. Ours. Jesus and his friends were making do with bread and wine, but the serving nuns had laid our places with large earthenware platters of *spaghetti alle vongole*, and were passing out bowls of grated Parmesan. The dishes were decorated in a creamy white slip with a pattern of blue dots around the rims. We had blue-checked cotton table napkins, which the Disciples did not, and raffia napkin-rings, and we had blue and white gingham tablecloths. Glass tumblers for our water, and thin stemmed glasses for our wine. This was robust and full-bodied, garnet-coloured, with an earthy taste of tannin. Delicious. This would be one for Michael all right. I could tell him about it, if I attended the *convegno* and was not too shy to approach him. We could discuss his wine researches, and I would have something to contribute. In the interest of connoisseurship I accepted a second glass.

After the *pastaciutta* we ate slices of grilled fennel with lemon, then green salad, ewe's milk cheese, and strawberries.

– All from the garden, Leonora said: except for the *vongole*. My cousin sent those, from Venice.

– And the sheep? I asked.

– They're out there, she said, waving a hand: out the back.

We were sitting together at a small table at the open end of the horseshoe of long tables. We all faced inwards, so that everyone could see everyone else. Grace was said in Italian by one of the novices, and then we all tucked in. No rule of silence here. No reading aloud of dreary holy books as at convent school. Supper was enlivened by conversation, joking and laughter.

After we had all finished, said another Grace, and processed out again, Leonora and I strolled in the cloister, smoking. It helped to keep the mosquitoes away. Leonora had given me a bottle of citronella earlier, but I had forgotten to dab any of the sweet-smelling liquid onto my face and neck. The mosquitoes followed me *en masse*, whining past my ears like fighter jets. Up and down we paced, in fragrant blue clouds of tobacco smoke.

Leonora discoursed on something she called *furta sacra*, which she had been reading about in a learned journal.

– It means sacred theft. In the Middle Ages everybody was at it. Basically, you had to have some relics, usually some bones, in order to inaugurate the altar in a new church. Bones of saints, I mean. I'm sure you know this. Well, if you didn't have any bones, you went and stole some. The more famous and the more powerful the better. Then you dedicated your church to the saint in question and lived under her protection. So the highways of Europe were full of caskets of dead saints being translated hither and thither. Saints were being ferried back and forth the entire time.

– So? I said.

She shrugged.

– So? I repeated: can I have another cigarette, please?

She lit fresh cigarettes for both of us and looked at me expectantly. This was the old Leonora, all right, tipping out her stories drop by drop, irritated if the audience lost patience or tried to hurry her up.

– Well, recently we've had a problem here. The local Bishop, a new appointee, has seen fit to suspend the saying of Mass in our chapel. I may add he hasn't been to visit us. He doesn't even speak to me. Everything is done by phone or email, through a secretary. He's a very conservative man, this Bishop, in fact completely reactionary as well as pigheaded. Completely hung up on lists. I had to fill in a form for him, by computer, listing all our assets. He noticed I didn't mention saints' relics. So having found out that in fact we had no relic of a saint under our altar, he declared our Masses invalid and had our Chaplain transferred elsewhere. Of course it's just an excuse. He wants to make trouble. Theologically I'm certain he's in error, particularly in this day and age, and I've filed a complaint against him with the Archbishop, but for the moment he has triumphed, and we can't have Mass said. So we have to go all the way down into town, using the steps. As you can imagine, for the older sisters, many of whom have rheumatism and arthritis, that's very hard.

– But why haven't you got any relics if all churches do? I asked.

– In our case, *cara*, our relics got lost, or you could say, indeed, translated, a long time ago. The Foundress disposed of all the relics that the first nuns brought with them as part of their dowries. She was being over-zealous and over-cautious, but hers was a new Foundation, and it was the time of the Counter-Reformation, and she didn't want to invite trouble by being seen to be superstitious. She entrusted the relics to one of the convent servants to hide down in the town, only unfortunately this woman removed the relics from underneath the altar as well. Nobody realised for a long time what she had done, and when they did find out they hushed it up. It would have looked bad for the convent, to be seen to have been so careless. Now, some time ago I discovered from the archives here in our library the name of the woman involved, and the date of the transfer of relics. The entry is very discreet. It just refers to some special washing for the Foundress. Do you remember that laundress whose life I began researching years ago in the local Inquisition records? I am certain she was the same woman.

– I do remember you telling me something about it, I said: you were very excited by her story. She was had up by the Inquisition for witchcraft but ultimately found innocent.

– Basically, Leonora explained: I've now realised the laundress was using the Brigandine relics to run a business, offering miraculous cures for infertility in return for cash. It's all there when you read between the lines. She did abortions too, as a sideline. And curses. She was making quite a lot of money. The Church couldn't be having that.

She looked at me. She was enjoying her recital. I just had to make the right appreciative noises.

– And so? I asked: what happened next?

– Well, *cara*, this is the miraculous bit. I found the rest of the record in Frederico's archive at the Museum, one day when I was there looking for something completely different. Goodness knows how it got there. It was a bundle of letters. It gave an address in Padenza. I went there and met the descendant of that laundress. Giovanna Schiavi, her name is. The mother of our own Sister Clara oddly enough. Hearing that we were in need of a saint's relic, she unlocked the box of relics from the cupboard in her house in which they had been kept safe all these years, and brought me the most beautiful one. The most ancient relic, and the most powerful. So we have been able to go ahead with our plans to have the chapel re-consecrated, without any problem.

– Ridiculous, I said: I'm not sure I believe a word of this. It's much too neat. Too many coincidences.

– Jung wouldn't call them coincidences, *cara*, Leonora said: he'd call them examples of synchronicity.

– You've been talking to Father Michael, I can tell, I said.

I drew deeply on my cigarette to give myself a pause for thought.

– You can still go to chapel to sing the Offices, I pointed out: isn't that enough? Couldn't the older nuns be content with that? Perhaps they'd be happy to be let off daily Mass, in any case. Surely the parish priest could nip up on Sundays and say Mass for you and bring a relic with him?

– No, *cara*. I have decided, and all our sisters agree with me, that if we are to become an internationally renowned pilgrimage site, as well as a major conference centre and retreat centre, then we must have a chapel where guests can not only pray but also, most importantly, attend Mass.

The Bishop has underestimated me. But once I present him with the evidence he'll have to come round. He wants a relic, I'll give him one.

– Very ambitious, your plans, I remarked.

– Of course, *tesoro*. It's all for the glory of God.

– So what relic is it that you're getting back? I asked: what saint? Is it the hand of Saint Briganda? Her toenail? Her nose?

– Don't mock, Leonora said.

She ground out her cigarette stub on the wall and put the stub in her pocket.

– Come and see, she said.

She led me out of the cloister, and up a staircase. We passed through a corridor of what I supposed were nuns' cells, their doors marked with Roman numerals, and turned a corner.

– It's under the bed at the moment, Leonora said: I couldn't think of anywhere safe to keep it.

She cocked her head on one side and put on a stagey voice. This was the Leonora of the seventies, acting her agit-prop, clothing her life in drama and mightily enjoying herself.

– It's so incredibly precious, and it's not insured. You wouldn't be able to get insurance for something like this. It's priceless.

Leonora's small cell was much plainer than my room in the guest wing. Its austerity and perfect proportions composed its beauty, the beamed wooden ceiling arching like a lid over flaking walls of rose plaster, a dusty floor of dark red tiles. Iron bed in one corner, covered with a blue blanket, table laden with books and laptop, a small chest, jug of wild daisies on the stone windowsill, a hook on the back of the door for dressing-gown, spare habit and jeans and T-shirt.

Leonora knelt down next to the bed and tugged out a flat cardboard box, of the sort that laundries used to send shirts back in. She stood up and came over to me, the box balanced delicately on her palms. She lifted off the lid.

All I could see was an oblong scrap of bleached white cloth, coarsely woven, ragged at the edges.

– It belonged to Saint Elizabeth, the friend of the Virgin, said Leonora: so it's even older than the Shroud of Turin.

Her voice was bland but her eyes sparkled with malice.

– Oh Leonora. I said: it's a fake. Of course it is. In any case, how can you, a reader of *Das Kapital*, believe in relics?

Leonora looked at me and sighed.

– You don't understand a thing, do you? Oh *cara*, don't you think it's ever so slightly intellectually lazy to speak in that way? It's not necessary for us to be concerned with literal truth in this instance. We are speaking of symbols, of the human need to create art celebrating the great turning points in our bodily lives.

I thought hazily of Father Michael's discourse, the evening we had drunk gin together. That was the problem with alcohol: the morning after you tended to have forgotten the clarifications of the night before.

– Oh, you mean like a metaphor?

– I said a symbol, *tesoro*. They are not exactly the same thing.

Leonora replaced the box under her bed. Then she stood up again and faced me.

– I must say I'm a little bit disappointed in your reaction, *cara*. I was expecting you to understand. The main point is that the stupid, reactionary, superstitious Bishop will accept this relic. See if he doesn't. And then I've got him. I'll expose him for the nincompoop he is. Believing simplistically in magic in this day and age. He'll look such a fool. He'll have to leave me alone after that.

She brushed the skirt of her habit, which was now patched with dust at knee level. Spiders' webs hung from her wide sleeves. She picked them off.

– I see that holy poverty includes not doing too much housework, I said.

Leonora pretended not to notice my irritated tone. She smiled. She had beautiful teeth: big and white. Her mouth was still as pink and plump as it had been in the seventies. Her face was smooth. That's nuns for you, Maude used to snort: of course they look young with the life they lead, no worries and no responsibilities. They're like children. They never grow up.

– Come to Vespers? Leonora suggested: you'll like it. We dance in the choir. It's what Saint Teresa of Avila's nuns did, to keep warm, but also to shake off the fleas. We are in the middle of summer, and we have no fleas, but still I think it's nice to dance.

— But what if the Bishop doesn't swallow your story? I asked: which is quite likely I should have thought. What will you do then?

— Then Plan B comes into operation, Leonora said: thanks to your help.

— B means bed for me, I said.

She kissed me.

— *Buona notte.* Sleep well, *tesoro.*

I did not see Leonora in the morning. Waking late and missing breakfast, I simply left her a note of thanks which I placed in the front hall on the table by the door. I scribbled I'd be in touch very shortly, and asked her to reserve me a place for the *convegno.* Then I walked down into town, my handbag in my arms.

The Museum was at the far end of the Piazza from the Caffe SS Pietro e Paulo. The building was a palazzo which had been turned into a bank and then into the town archive. Twenty years ago it had been transformed into a museum, with the archive kept in a room on the *piano nobile.*

Italian palaces had surprised me on my first trip to Italy with Cecil. We'd gone to Florence for him to measure up some tombs. Although Cecil discoursed on the palazzi lining the Florentine streets I couldn't recognise them. Blank stone façades reared up above me. One next to another like houses in a London terrace. I'd thought he meant palaces like Buckingham Palace or in Walt Disney, with space around them, and pinnacles, and turrets. I quickly grew to know better. At night I studied manuals on the mathematics and history of architecture and tried to commit the terms to memory. I recited them like the Catechism. But alas I didn't have the terms for successful marriage in my mind and they turned out to be just as important.

Frederico met me under the portico as we had arranged. The Ionic capitals on the columns were perfect. Definitely Balladian.

– I won't offer you a guided tour today, Frederico said: in any case you've seen the galleries before, when you were here with Cecil, I'm sure.

– Yes, I said: although I shall certainly take another look at some point. I can't remember the half of what you've got.

– I haven't got time to show you around this morning, Frederico said: I am sorry. I am so busy. But I'll show you the flat, and how the keys work, and the alarm, and so on. Oh, don't worry. The flat is on a separate alarm system. We have guards who patrol at night. You will be quite safe, even if a burglar comes.

He led me through the entrance doors into the vestibule, and across a wide marble-floored entry hall. Tourists and schoolchildren wandered to and fro. Racks of leaflets and sets of headphones flanked the ticket desk, a glassed-in kiosk. Opposite stood a bookstall, stands of postcards. To one side a blank screen was labelled Schools Textiles Exhibition.

– That's our outreach work, Frederico said: the local students are putting together their own project to complement our exhibition. They're as behind as we are.

He pointed towards a pair of wooden doors inside a painted wooden doorframe.

– Through there, down the staircase at the end of that gallery, is the basement, which I am turning into a restoration workshop. I've had the attics cleared out, so that we can use them as a storage space for paintings not currently on show, and I have brought down all the broken artefacts into the basement. There's a great deal of restoration work to be done. Paintings, statues, sculptures, pots, all kinds of things.

– I dislike broken things hanging around myself, I said: when I break something either I mend it or I throw it out immediately.

– I don't want the Museum to be a mortuary, Frederico said: I'd rather it were a hotel, or at a pinch a hospital, but definitely not a mortuary.

He swept me up the grand vaulted staircase that rose from the back of the entrance hall. This lofty tunnel of stone reared up, turned a corner at right angles, and then another. Halfway up, Frederico opened a side door on the landing, and ushered me in. We walked through a large salon, fitted up as an office with a baize-topped table, leather armchairs, old-fashioned steel filing cabinets.

– This is where I used to work. But I've had a new studio made, in part of the *piano nobile*. What used to be the archive has now become the office, and most of the archive has been moved to bigger and airier premises upstairs. This room is disused at the moment. Come, here's the flat.

He unlocked a door at the far end.

– Now, I hope this will be all right. Very tiny as you see. Very basic.

Open doors off the narrow vestibule gave onto a bathroom on one side, a kitchenette on the other. Super-modern: the bathroom all grey concrete floors and walls, with a grey concrete basin and hipbath, and the kitchen all steel. At the end of the short passage we erupted into a dark room. Frederico stepped to the window, and pushed aside the shutter a little way, letting in a shaft of light. Whiteness settled on a graceful oval table and two chairs, a sofa with scrolled ends, a couple of display cabinets, a writing-table under the window. Two vast oil paintings hung opposite each other on the damask-covered walls. A steep little ladder-like staircase led up to a platform with a bed on it. I peered through the glass doors of the cabinet nearest me at some bronze figurines of gods. Eros and Bacchus and Apollo.

– These must be artefacts from the collection, I said: oh my goodness.

– Well, Frederico said: there's not much point being the Director if I can't have some nice objects to look at, is there? Don't worry, these aren't among our most precious items. I thought you might like to live amongst them for a little while, so I shan't have them taken away.

He showed me how to lock the outer door and set the alarm.

– Paolo downstairs, the guardian on duty, he knows you're here, and will do anything he can to help you. Just ask him for anything you need. Here's my office telephone number, and the number of my mobile. You've got a mobile?

– Yes, I said.

– Good. I'll see you tomorrow night, downstairs, at seven. *Ciao.*

He kissed me on both cheeks and darted off.

I unpacked. I put my toothpaste in the bathroom, my set of clean underwear in the top drawer of a little eighteenth-century chest, and the gold canister on the shelf in the kitchen. I glanced at the vast oil paintings. Their narratives ran in strips, picture sequences like those of modern cartoons. One painting depicted the legend of Psyche and the other the legend of Persephone. A nymph, and the daughter of a goddess. Both were dressed in High Renaissance style. They wore gold sandals fastened with gold laces wrapped about their ankles, sleeveless pleated tunics belted with jewels, long gauzy scarves, and tiny caps of gold mesh perched on the backs of their heads. I decided to go out and buy some goddessy clothes.

First of all, though, some fresh air. I wrestled with the anti-mosquito square of mesh in its wooden frame, and managed to lift this off. Then I tackled the window catch, tugged the stiff window open. Finally I folded back the half-open metal shutter, which wrinkled like a concertina, as far as it would go. The window was a wide, low slit. I leaned my elbows on the windowsill and snuffed up the smell of fresh bread and oranges and dust and sun-warmed stone. I remembered I was on the mezzanine, just above the capitals of the columns and pilasters of the entrance. If I could have put my arm out far enough I would presumably have been able to touch them. But the little aperture in the stone wall was far too deep to let me get my hand out that far.

The sounds of the outside surged into the room: motorbikes revving, people calling, a bell beginning to ring the noon Angelus. The hour was later than I had thought. The shops would soon be closing. I seized my wallet, turned back to seal the window again. Beyond it I could see the capitals of the church opposite, the attic storey of the café next to it. You couldn't see the ground. Just a streak of luminous blue sky above the café roof.

A piercing female voice began exclaiming in English down in the street.

– Quite draughty, you'd think, with no proper front door.

A second, equally loud, replied.

– It looks like a railway station, doesn't it?

Edmund's reproachful tones swatted these comments aside.

– This palazzo, ladies, is one of Balladio's masterpieces. Note the severe restraint of the capitals emphasizing the purity of the architrave which conceals the grainstore hidden behind in the mezzanine.

I realised he was directing his companions' eyes towards the very room in which I stood. I felt like a secret, which the Museum was keeping, my name a word which its stone lips were not yet ready to utter.

– Alas, the Museum appears to be closing for lunch, Edmund said: how sad. I had hoped we could view together the newly opened gallery of textiles. But it was not to be. Another time, dear ladies.

Their voices receded. I waited a few minutes, and then crept downstairs. I found the back exit Frederico had told me about, pushed open the squeaking door, and erupted into a courtyard full of thin cats. A thin man was leaning against a column, smoking, watching the cats dance about the scraps he had obviously just put down for them.

– *Signora*, he said, shaking my hand: have you got everything you need? Do you know where to go? Do you know where all the restaurants are?

– Yes, thank you, I said: I do. What would you say are the specialities of the season? What would you recommend I try?

– Donkey stew is always very nice, he said: or grilled slices of polenta, or *baccala*.

– Fine, I said: I'll have the lot.

I was a widow going out to lunch on her own in one of the most beautiful cities in Italy. I was alone, and independent, and OK, and hungry. I trotted happily along the street. I knew I was about to have a really wonderful time.

My mobile rang.

– Oh, *cara*, could you possibly give me a hand? Leonora asked: I completely forgot to ask you last night. It's for the *convegno*. I can't manage without you. Could you come back up right away and help me out? Are you any good on ladders? I'll explain when I see you. I won't say more now. Just in case the Bishop is tapping my phone. It's just a spot of DIY.

– Can't you get one of the nuns to do it? I asked: heights scare me, rather. I might become vertiginous and fall off.

– Just a short ladder, Leonora said: I'll hold it in case it wobbles.

Lunch receded. Maude would have approved. Skipping meals was so good for the waistline.

– Oh, all right then, I said.

CHAPTER FOUR

The following morning, my eyes, gummed shut by crusty green sleep and pus, would not open. Stuck fast. Trying to crack this glue felt like prising apart the two halves of a walnut shell with a single fingernail. At last I managed it. The surrounding flesh had swollen up so that I could scarcely see. A mistake, in any case, to glance in the mirror. The face that shrieked back was unrecognisable as mine: a mask of red lumps, eyelids inflated like over-pumped-up rubber tyres. My neck was likewise covered with bites, and my arms and hands: any part of me that had protruded from beneath the sheet during the night. I looked grotesque. Monstrous. The mosquito bites throbbed and itched; a concerto of scratchiness. I wanted to burst into tears, but forbade myself: it would hurt too much.

I put on my dark glasses, my tired black trouser-suit, and crept out of the little flat. I locked the door of the outer room behind me, as Frederico had shown me, and put out my hand to de-activate the alarm while I got downstairs. I prepared to tiptoe through a secret, shuttered space: the Museum would not open for another hour.

How odd. The alarm light showed Off. Yet surely I'd left it on last night?

Some kind of change in the light jumped me alert. I stiffened. Movement. A presence. The hairs rose on the back of my neck.

I felt trapped, in what had become, suddenly, an uncanny place, with no way out. Something shivery and cold hovered and waited. I gripped my keyring and stared doggedly at the keyhole in front of me. If I pretended nothing was happening then I could escape.

I heard a rustle, and forced myself to glance up.

A ripple of blue. A tall woman, her black hair in elaborate ringlets. She wore a long, spreading bulk of blue pleats: an antique dress in a shape so stiff it seemed carved. She drifted across the landing above me, at the right-angled turn of the wide stairs. The mask of her powdered white face gleamed above the starched lace collar embracing her bare shoulders.

She paused, as though she sensed me gaping, then gathered her hands into the deep folds of her gown, lifted and bunched them, put out a foot in a red high-heeled shoe.

My hands flew to my mouth in case I screeched. Supposing she decided to come closer. Supposing she tried to touch me?

Her expressionless, half-hooded eyes looked through me, made me invisible. She began her descent.

Fear sloshed inside me, chilled my stomach, impelled flight. I stumbled downstairs ahead of the visitant in blue,

knees shaking. My feverish state had induced an appari-
tion. Or perhaps, as I'd feared in London, I was indeed
going crazy. I'd never imagined I'd seen a ghost before. I'm
an extrovert, I insisted to myself: I do not believe in ghosts.
This vision comes from a sleepless night and too much
scratching.

At the bottom of the stairs I paused and looked back.
The empty air danced with motes of dust.

I left the Museum by the back entrance, and slunk into
the café on the corner for a cappuccino. The woman
behind the counter clucked when she saw my face.

– Oh, poor *Signora*.

She gave me a *jetone*, and I rang Leonora. The bites hurt
worse than ever. I began sobbing, with pain, with humil-
iation, with heat. I seemed to have turned into one
inflamed ulcerous wound.

– Oh, *cara*, poor you, Leonora cried: I forgot to make
sure you took the citronella with you when you left. I'm so
sorry. I'll send Sister Clara down straight away with some
ointment and some medicine. Where will she find you?

– I'll be in the Caffe Elizabetta, I croaked.

– Don't worry, *cara*, help is on its way. Thank you again
for all your hard work yesterday. I appreciate it very much.

I had spent the entire afternoon in the cloister, rigging
up, under Leonora's instructions, the wire along which a
cardboard replica of the Annunciation dove was due to fly
to mark the opening of the *convegno*.

Leonora had pinched the idea from the Easter Sunday

ceremony in Florence, which Cecil had once taken me to witness. The officiating prelate, standing at the High Altar of the cathedral, lit the touch paper on the firework-dove's tail. This Florentine dove, possibly symbolising the Holy Ghost, if I correctly remembered Cecil's exegesis, whizzed down the aisle on its invisible wire, out of the huge doors at the back, specially opened for the occasion, and smashed into a cart of fireworks which duly erupted in flames. Then white oxen in decorated harness came to tow the cart away.

In Leonora's version the dove would fly the other way, from outdoors towards indoors, to make the symbolism of the Annunciation clearer.

– The Virgin's ear, *cara*, can be perceived as a symbol of a sexual orifice. Is that why language can have such an erotic effect on a listener? Is that related to concepts of Muses operating as fantasy lovers to inspire baby-books?

– Men get pregnant too? I asked.

– Obviously. We shall discuss all this at the *convegno*, among other topics.

Thinking of Michael's deep voice caressing my earlobes I shuddered all over, and nearly dropped my hammer.

– You've got a Virgin for the dove to penetrate? I enquired from the top of my ladder.

– Certainly. You're going to nail her up for me in a moment, just here outside the chapel door.

-And the white oxen?

-We haven't any, Leonora said: I don't want to overdo it.

I wished the mosquitoes of the Padentine night had heeded similar advice. Itching and scratching, I drank my cappuccino in the darkest corner of the *caffe*, then braved the street. Merely keeping my head down did not sufficiently conceal me from the pitying or amused stares of passersby. I needed to cover myself; to hide completely. With gratitude I noticed the trader further along, busy setting out his stall of beads, necklaces, belts and bolts of cloth. When I approached, paused to look over his wares, he too clicked his teeth.

– Oh, poor *Signora*.

I inspected his brightly coloured batiks. I wanted black draperies but there were none. Purple whorls on green, and red diamonds on blue, would have to suffice.

– I don't think those colours are quite you, somehow, the stallholder said: forgive my mentioning it.

– They'll do, I snapped, opening my purse.

He shook his head.

– Oh, you English. What colour sense.

Retiring into the alleyway nearby, I draped one cloth over my head and wound the other around my waist. I undid the zip of my hateful black trousers, shook them off, and dumped them into a conveniently-placed waste bin. Now at least I felt a little cooler, without the clinging fabric irritating my over-sensitive skin. Now the morning heat could stroke the bites on my calves and ankles.

Last night I had eaten outside at the pizzeria in Contra S. Angelo, not realising what a lure I represented to all the fanged beasts of the vicinity; what a challenge. While I bit into pizza with artichokes they bit into my ankles. I couldn't see them: they pierced me stealthily. Too late, each time I felt the nip, put my hand down, checked the inflamed place, already swelling into an unbearable bump, rubbed until I broke the skin, drew a little blood. Relief, plus the promise of a big red scab which would take weeks to heal.

Back in the little flat matters got worse. I had left the shutter open when I went out, assuming the fine grille over the windows would keep insects at bay. Wrong. A bloodthirsty mosquito can break and enter anywhere. Throughout the hours of darkness I tossed and turned, scratching. Predators screamed past my ears, diving in for the kill. Each time I felt bitten I turned on the light and sat up, to spot the vampire insect, plump and sated, panting, boldly sitting on the wall next to me. Practically grinning at my distress. I smashed each one with a shoe. My blood spattered the cream damask wallpaper as the mosquitoes burst under the impact of my Clarks heel. By morning, sleepless, covered in seeping ulcers, I'd been transformed into one great twitching lump of misery, and the wall bore mute red witness to serial killing.

Arriving, for my rendezvous with Sister Clara, at the Caffe Elizabetta, I could not bear either to go in or to sit outside. If I asked the waiter to bring me some mineral water he might laugh, or turn me away as a bad advertisement for his establishment. My swollen, ugly face might chase away potential customers. I loitered beside the statue of Balladio's wife, head well down, hands clutched together to keep from attacking my red weals. I scanned the passersby for any hint of a nun's habit. Sister Clara, where are you? Oh, please hurry.

The citizens were all out and about, taking the morning air. Fathers sauntered, pushing toddlers in strollers. Bicycles, ridden by mothers who had popped their babies, propped on pillows, into their handlebar-baskets, wobbled past. Early morning shoppers clutched paper bags of breakfast buns and whistled as they walked. Some of them glanced at me as they passed, and shrugged. The sun beat the crown of my head through its cotton covering. I longed to be indoors, somewhere dark and cool. Preferably to be unconscious. Anaesthetized. Even dead.

– And yet in a rich place like this, in the north of Italy, you can still see the most terrible poverty, the most terrible human wretchedness. It's shocking, really.

Maude's voice. Coming from behind me, from the shady arcade that wrapped the south side of the Basilica. Cautiously I turned my head and peeped into the dimness. There she stood, ten yards distant, clad in a purple silk sundress and white straw hat, holding a camera in one hand, turning her head to address her two companions. Maude! She was supposed to be safely at home in Greenhill, pasting her pilgrimage snaps into her holiday album, not gallivanting around the Veneto. I shrank further into myself. I absolutely did not want to have to deal with her. Go away, I implored her silently: buzz off like a mosquito and bite someone else.

Maude's tones rang out clear and loud, as those of the English abroad so often do. That middle-class accent: so piercing and confident, so strident compared to the dark stream, the guttural opera, of Italians talking to one another. How could she be so noisy? Everybody would be turning to look at her. The Padentines, unable to avoid hearing her, would glance at each other, give that twitch of the eyebrow that meant: oh, tourists; and continue on their way. I could never bear to speak English in public in Italy. If I had to do so, I whispered. I didn't want to stand out and be noticeable. I wanted to merge, to vanish into the throng. To pass, if at all possible, for Italian. Today, more than ever, I wanted to be invisible. Difficult, when you're wrapped mummy-like in shrieking colours, and your flesh has melted to a mass of crimson suppuration.

– Just look at that poor creature begging over there. Covered in putrefying sores. Some terrible disease, I suppose. Leprosy do you think? I suppose we should give her something, but, really, she is so disgusting. Poor thing.

Two men accompanied Maude. One, of medium height, plump and red-faced, dressed in grey crimplene, carried a panama hat and a large pink handkerchief with which he wiped his brow. Father Kenneth. The other, tall, grey-haired, with a big nose and a humorous mouth, wore a white T-shirt and black jeans, carried a black leather biker's jacket tossed over one shoulder. How handsome

Father Michael looked once out of his priestly gear. What a revelation of the real person beneath the polyester disguise. He looked like a man now, not a bureaucrat. I gawped at him through the misery of my bites. How brown and muscular his arms. He glanced at me, and his eyes narrowed. I nearly yelped with horror. Quickly I hunched my shoulders and scowled, tried to look even more like a person with a horrid affliction than I already did. It wasn't difficult: pain shook me, saturated me like a special form of heat. I wanted to burst into hysterical tears.

Just at that moment someone laid a hand on my arm. I turned. A young woman with a blonde crewcut and big blue eyes smiled at me. She wore a white sweatshirt with the slogan Brigandines printed across the bosom, white jeans and white trainers, and she carried a yellow leather satchel.

– So sorry to have kept you waiting. Oh, poor *Signora*. You've had a terrible reaction to the bites, haven't you? These are what we call tropical ulcers. You don't often see them this far north. Come with me. Let's go somewhere quiet and I can attend to you.

Maude and her two companions wandered away, shaking their heads and sighing. They vanished from sight in the crowd of passersby. Sister Clara pulled me round the corner, down the narrow flight of stone steps clinging to the side of the Basilica, and into Piazza delle Erbe. She sat me down on a bollard outside a wine shop.

– Here will do fine.

She opened her satchel.

– No time to lose. Here we are. I'll just pat on some of this lotion and you'll start to feel better immediately, I promise.

Unscrewing the cap of a little green bottle, she wetted a piece of cottonwool with some of the liquid it contained and dabbed at my bites. Instant impact. As though she were applying bolts of coolness to my insides. I shuddered as the pain fled from me. I felt weak, and close to tears again.

She crouched, applying the soothing balm to my ankles and calves. I shivered as the coldness hit the bites, seemed to penetrate me to the quick. I sighed.

– I can't tell you how good that feels. Where did you learn to make such potions? You're a witch.

– Oh, Sister Clara said: it runs in the family.

She produced a second bottle, untwisted its stopper, drew out a little rubber-tipped dropper.

– Here. I'm going to put some of this on your tongue. Open wide.

The liquid tasted bitter. I grimaced and swallowed.

– What is it?

– A mild herbal tranquillizer. It will help you to stay calm while the lotion works on the bites, so that you won't be tempted to scratch.

She put her hands on her hips and studied me.

– Right. Now the next thing we have to do is get you some decent clothes. That's what Leonora said, and I must say I think she is right. You English! Your colour sense is really extraordinary. In Italy we love colours but you don't have to overdo it.

— Now? I protested: but I can't go into a shop looking like this.

— Believe me, Sister Clara said: you will feel a whole lot better once you have got something nice to wear. Come along. We're going to my aunt's boutique in Corso Balladio. She'll give us a good discount. She provides us with all our clothes for the convent. That's where my sweatshirt came from. D'you like it?

She spun around, arms wide, a carousel nun.

— I didn't realise some of you wore lay clothes, I said.

She took my arm and began to march me out of Piazza delle Erbe by the back way.

— Oh, she said: we all wear ordinary clothes to come into town. It wouldn't do to come down wearing our habits. They're much too old-fashioned. They would draw attention to us in a way we wouldn't like. We wear habits up at the convent because we enjoy it. But they're a form of fancy-dress really. We don't like the modern habits the Bishop recommends to us. Too ugly. The one thing we simply will not wear is polyester.

The plate-glass window of her aunt's boutique displayed wildly fantastical summer frocks in wispy chiffon decorated with feathers and sequins. In we went. The aunt, in a skimpy white linen suit sewn with gold glass beads and gold high-heeled sandals, embraced Clara. She clucked when she saw me sidling in after her niece.

– Oh, poor *Signora*.

She understood immediately what we wanted. In a moment she had me kitted out in a calf-length scarlet shift in very thin silk, which floated lightly over my bites. These, thanks to the calming medicine, had begun to subside, already looked much less raised and angry.

– There, *Signora*, Clara said: now you look pretty and nice.

– Oh, for heaven's sake, I said: you've saved my life, call me Aurora.

Clara insisted I buy a second dress, a sleeveless tube in indigo linen, flatteringly cut, plus a black, green and white striped skirt, ankle-length, gathered very full, and a white silk and chiffon T-shirt to go with it.

– Everything else you need you can get in the market tomorrow. They have lovely clothes, very cheap.

The aunt did not seem to mind the recommendation of a rival establishment. She nodded vigorously.

– Certainly. Now let me just wrap these up.

She embraced Clara and shook me by the hand.

– Come and see me again. I have lots of things I think you will like.

Back in the Piazza I tried to thank Clara, and to offer her a cup of coffee. She shook her head. She opened her satchel, took out the two little bottles, and pressed them upon me. She gave me a pot of citronella ointment too, and a packet of citronella mosquito spirals.

– Just doing my job. Thank you, but I must get back.

Have these. You ought to return to your room now and reapply the ointment and take some more drops. Every two hours. And make sure to rest. By tonight all the bite-marks should have vanished. *Ciao*, Aurora.

We kissed each other. She whirled off. I donned my sunglasses and strolled across Piazza dei Signori with my head up and my shoulders back, a glossy carrier bag in each hand. I enjoyed the cool swish of silk over my knees. I enjoyed going along in dark glasses. I could see people but they couldn't see me.

– Dawn! Is that really you?

– Well, hello there, Delphine!

– Hello, Aurora.

Maude, arms akimbo, blocked my passage, staring. The two priests flanked her, one on each side of her, posed as erect as bodyguards.

– What on earth have you done to your face? Maude cried: and I must say, darling, I should never have said that red was really your colour. Isn't the cut of that frock just a weeny bit too young?

– Oh, hello, Maude, I said: hello, Father Michael. Father Kenneth.

I described the encounter later on to Frederico, as we sped out of town in his little emerald sports car. I didn't tell him about the mosquito bites, for fear he should think I was criticising his hospitality. Perhaps the Museum even took a certain pride in its mosquitoes, who knows? They came with the antiquities, and the painting of Psyche performing her heroic tasks, and the noisy plumbing, and the bath-tap that only dripped, rather than gushed, when you turned it on. I had found a plastic jug in the kitchenette, had set it to fill, and had enjoyed my makeshift shower very much. Bathed in magical Clara-lotion, I had lain down for a siesta, cool skin gliding between cool sheets. Exhausted by lack of sleep the previous night, I slept all afternoon.

The Angelus bells rang just outside. I awoke, miraculously weal-free, and very hungry. I had forgotten to have lunch. I jumped up, poured another jugful of water over myself, donned the black, green and white striped skirt, and the white chiffon T-shirt. I put on the shoes I had bought on the way home: flat green satin slippers tied with black ribbons. There wasn't enough water to wash my hair so I piled it up in a rough chignon. I threaded the long spikes of my silver earrings through the holes in my earlobes, splashed myself with eau de Cologne. In my handbag I took the pot of citronella. Just in case. Perhaps Frederico's house would have no anti-mosquito protection. Perhaps Padentine mosquitoes only bit foreigners. Perhaps even now the troops were massing, lying in wait, rubbing their proboses together in sadistic anticipation of a succulent suck.

– How lovely you look this evening, Aurora, Frederico said, handing me into the car: so cool and fresh. I think Padenza must suit you.

He revved and reversed. We shot backwards out of the

Museum carpark straight into the traffic. Horns beeped and tyres screeched. A policeman's whistle blew. Frederico made an exasperated gesture, swore, executed a swift turn, and we roared away over the bridge, heading for the main road out of town.

– It does, I said: except for Maude's arrival. She says she had such a good time in Rome she couldn't bear to go home, so she decided to come on to Padenza and surprise me, and Father Kenneth felt he ought to accompany her, to make sure she'd be all right.

I didn't know what Father Michael thought he was up to, tagging along. Oh yes, I remembered now. Research on wines. A conscientious trawl through the provincial vineyards. I wished him joy. He'd hardly spoken to me when we all met earlier. Just stood there looking distant and cool while Maude rabbited on.

– I know it's very mean of me, I said: but I didn't want my stepmother here. I wanted a holiday all by myself.

– But tell me, Frederico said, steering with his knees while he lit a cigarette and tossed the match out of the window: should I have invited her tonight? Perhaps, nonetheless, she wanted your company? She's your family, after all.

– No, I said: she's going to the cinema. She's going to see a documentary film on Padre Pio with Father Kenneth that's on at some Catholic youth centre or other he's discovered. Then she said she's going to have an early night. She'll be fine.

We sped out of the city and through the villages on its outskirts, now woven into the urban fabric as pretty, countrified suburbs. Rapidly leaving these behind, we erupted into the real countryside, the Veneto plain stretching all around. We ran under a tunnel of plane trees. Red-roofed houses dotted the landscape stretching away from the road. Neat market-gardens brimmed with rows of blue wrinkled cabbages striping the rich brown of the earth. Flowering creepers, purple and pink, covered sheds and fences.

– Now, Frederico said: what music shall we have on? The CDs are in that pocket there, just in front of you. Please choose one.

I selected the Bach *Magnificat*. He played it very loud as we rushed down the quiet country road. A dry riverbed twisted alongside. Misty blue distances surrounded us, sky merging into mountains. We fled through gold-bronze maize fields, the spears rustling waist-high. The mountains came closer, their flanks pink in the setting sun. Walls of rock feathered with pines. Frederico had rolled down the top of the car, so that the air could come in; humid; pushing past our faces. The golden evening smelled of hay, and of river-water.

– This morning I felt very melancholy, Frederico said: but now I feel better.

– English people often think Italians are always merry and singing and so on, I said: but in my experience they are often melancholy.

– It's because we think so much, Frederico said: I dreamed about God last night. A pair of fiery red eyes hidden in a cloud, glaring at me. The Ark sailed into the cloud and when it came out the other side all the animals were painted different colours.

– Like a sort of celestial car-wash, I said.

– Exactly, Frederico said.

He sang aloud with the choir. *Magnificat! Magnificat!* I joined in. He turned his head towards me, smiling, and we sang loudly to each other above the roar and bang of the little car.

– You've not been to my house before, Frederico asked, as the music finished: have you?

– No, I said: Cecil always used to visit you on his own. He came to see you for business meetings.

– Oh dear, Frederico said: I am afraid they were dinner parties nonetheless. He always said you were too busy studying to come out. I was terribly in awe of you, doing so much studying while we were larking about drinking wine and gossiping.

– It's not a dinner party tonight, though, is it? I asked.

– No, no, Frederico reassured me: nothing formal at all. It's just us and my mother and sister and a few friends.

Italian definitions sometimes differed from English ones. I remembered travelling with Cecil one July to the Cinque Terre on the Tuscan coast, Frederico having assured him that it was a completely deserted spot, perfect for the relaxation Cecil needed from his labours in the archive. Of course it swarmed with Italians sunbathing, strolling, sitting, drinking, playing ball, running about, swimming, eating, chatting, and generally having a lovely time. Cecil's nerves could not stand the crowd and the commotion. We had to leave immediately.

We turned off the road and swerved right, up a narrow track between high stone walls, into a tiny cobbled square. At the far side of this, iron gates, backed with sheets of tin, confronted us, set into a stone wall topped with statues of female dwarves. Beyond, one could just see a grey oblong: the top storey of the house, a row of dark red squares of wood patching its length. A small tower lifted up at one end, a loggia tucked under its red-tiled roof.

– It used to be a convent, Frederico said: hence a certain austerity of design. I rather like its plainness.

He tooted his horn. A dog began baying. Above us shutters crashed back and a window flew open. A teenaged girl stuck her head out. She was dark-haired and olive-skinned, and had the same narrow, handsome face as Frederico.

– I'm coming, she shrieked.

She vanished.

– My niece Rosamaria, Frederico said: aged fourteen. The daughter of my sister Francesca.

The gates parted. A smiling Rosamaria poked her face out. She tugged the gates open from the inside. She gave a mock salute as we edged forwards. Dressed in a smart navy skirt and a short-sleeved white blouse, her school uniform, perhaps, she looked very young. We rolled in over the crunching gravel, past a clump of ancient magnolias, around the side of the house to a cobbled yard.

– Used to be the stables, Frederico said.

No horses stuck their heads out over the half-doors. Their quarters now housed sheds and garages. The air smelled not of horse manure but of petrol.

– I'll put the car away, Frederico said: because later on we'll organise you a taxi for getting back. Come in and meet my family. But first we'll go in through the kitchen and say hello to Giovanna.

Rosy copper cake moulds bloomed on a high mantel-piece over a big black stove. A tall, fine-featured woman, her dark hair in a bun, turned from the range, hid her smile under a frown. She wore a blue check overall and a white apron, shook a black frying pan over the flame. The scent of mushrooms and olive oil rushed into my nostrils.

– Giovanna is married to Paolo, one of the watchmen at the Museum, whom I think you've already met, Frederico explained: she is very kindly helping us out tonight. Normally I do the cooking, because my mother doesn't know how.

Giovanna nodded at me and lifted a finger at Frederico.

– You're late. If dinner's spoiled it'll be all your fault.

– Oh, oh, Frederico exclaimed: we'll hurry, then.

A pair of black wooden doors, seeming very low in the high wall, split apart to take us into the hall. From there we darted through a complicated succession of corridors, anterooms and rooms, one opening out of another. I trod over silk rugs, gleaming marble. Just as I became completely bewildered and lost we entered a final salon, so dark that I couldn't distinguish the people in it from the furniture. A sea of misty grey shapes, like an interior by Whistler. Gradually my eyes adjusted to the dim light.

The group of human profiles turned towards me. They swam against panelled, grey-painted walls hung with pictures, photographs, swords in scabbards, the masks of foxes and deer. A mirror of spotted Venetian glass in an engraved glass frame tilted above an ornate grey marble fireplace. Armchairs upholstered in grey and yellow satin lined the walls. Boxes, bowls, dishes and statues covered the surfaces of ormolu tables. The tall windows had curtains pulled across them. Perhaps to keep out the mosquitoes. Good.

– My mother insists on leaving everything exactly as it was when she was a child, Frederico said, waving at the massed ornaments: she wants to keep her memories precise and intact. If she so much as moves a pincushion by a single centimetre she is convinced something awful will happen. I tell her that's not how to run a museum but she won't listen.

Contessa Pagan squeezed my hands in hers, then kissed me on both cheeks. She was a small woman, with wavy fair hair. She wore a grey linen suit. Beautifully cut.

– Be quiet, Frederico. Welcome, dear Aurora. What a pleasure to see you again.

I remembered her from an opening twenty years ago at the Museum. The bigwigs had scared me but she had been kind. We had discussed clothes, and she had confessed to a weakness for the shops in Milan. Now she introduced me to her daughter Francesca and the latter's husband, the local doctor and his wife, a couple of male cousins. Too many names to remember. I sorted them by their costumes. Francesca took first prize. She wore a conical-shaped cream lace dress, which complemented her conical black top-knot. She carried a gold canister, exactly like mine, as a handbag. We were bound to get on, I thought. Perhaps later in the evening we could compare canisters. The other woman was in ribbed fuchsia satin. The men wore silk suits.

– And this is—

Father Michael got up from an antique chair. I caught a glimpse of pale pink socks. He stepped forward. He had changed before coming out. He had put on dark blue linen trousers that matched his eyes, left his white cotton shirt open at the neck. You could see a hint of collarbone, that tender hollow. A little shiver of bliss erupted in my throat.

– We know each other. Hello again, Aurora.

Kissing seemed to be catching. He kissed me gravely on both cheeks. He smelled of Eau Sauvage. I wanted to kiss him back, not on both cheeks but on the mouth, but I restrained myself. He smiled at me.

– What a coincidence, I said: that we should bump into each other again so soon.

– Jung wouldn't say coincidence so much as synchronicity, he said.

– Oh yes, I said, feeling foolish: I remember now. Leonora was mentioning synchronicity only yesterday.

– Padenza is a small town, you were bound to meet, Contessa Pagan said: everybody in Padenza knows everybody else, and in the art history world it's presumably the same, isn't it?

Frederico handed me a glass of prosecco.

– Michael's giving the opening talk tomorrow at the *convegno*, so I thought it would be nice to invite him to dinner with us and get to know him. I invited Leonora too, but she didn't want to come out. The Bishop's got his eye on her and she's got to be seen to behave. He wants to close the convent down. Any excuse will do.

– Can he do that? I asked.

– Oh yes. He's the boss of the diocese. The Brigandines are too independent for him. They question his authority and that displeases him. It's a fight to the death between him and Leonora. She likes a good fight, of course. But she might lose this one.

– The Bishop is a rather old-fashioned person, Contessa Pagan said to me: he is wary of progress.

Someone beat a gong vigorously just outside.

– Oh dear, the Contessa exclaimed: the risotto mustn't be kept sitting too long. Let's take our drinks in with us.

Rosamaria, will you show Aurora where she can wash her hands, and then go to help Giovanna?

I followed Rosamaria back through the twist of ante-rooms to the front hall. Here we halted. She pointed at a little door in the panelling.

– In there. Those used to be cupboards, but my uncle converted them.

– Thank you, I said.

– Are you a friend of Leonora's? Rosamaria asked: she's my godmother. I'm designing a website for the convent. Do you like computers? Have you got a website?

– I use a computer for my VAT returns, I said: and I really ought to have a website. What a good idea.

– I'll design you one if you like, Rosamaria said: I can see you enjoy Italian style. I like your shoes.

She smiled at me. She waved a hand, and darted off.

On the other side of the small door I found an old-fashioned bathroom. The lavatory had a wooden seat, a cistern high up on the wall. The taps on the wash basin were heavy brass. A mirrored shelf, acting as dressing-table, held a hairbrush and comb, a stack of little embossed linen towels, a flask of eau de Cologne.

I emerged to find Frederico waiting for me.

– I thought I'd come and show you the way to the dining-room. It's easy to get lost in this house. From the outside it looks like a simple oblong but the interior is almost circular. When it was re-built, turned from a con-vent into a villa, the owner, the same woman who founded

Leonora's Order, she had it re-designed to have an oval suite of rooms, following the design of Balladio's Basta-Rotunda. Her architect was very keen on Balladio.

– It does seem to go round and round, I said: I thought it was just me not knowing my left from my right.

– All the rooms lead back to the bedroom at its heart, Frederico said: oh yes, the bedroom was on the ground floor. It's now our dining-room. Rather confusing, isn't it?

– Your house reminds me of one of the sections of that painting of Psyche in your flat in the Museum, I said: I mean of Eros's palace when she arrives there.

– Good, said Frederico: I am pleased. I seem to remember she was given delicious food. That's always a good beginning, isn't it?

He swept us through a final pair of double doors into the dining-room, which, lit by a single chandelier, was almost as dark as the salon. We sat on velvet armchairs at a big oval table covered by a white cloth, our knees swathed in heavy white napkins, a row of glasses lined up in front of each place. Giovanna, who stayed hidden out of sight in the kitchen, like Eros's invisible servants, sent in our dinner via Rosamaria. Like a little whirlwind the teenager darted about, carrying dishes and plates.

Over the first course the discussion of local politics, and of the Bishop in particular, went passionately on, aided by some excellent wine. This unlabelled white, from the family's vineyard, accompanied our plates of risotto. The fat, buttery rice had melting cubes of sharp blue cheese stirred into it, and came decorated with crisp fried sage leaves.

– That Bishop, snorted the elder of Frederico's cousins, who was sitting on one side of me: I was at school with him, and he was a bully even then. He was unbelievably reactionary and sentimental. We did military service together, that was before he became a priest of course, and I remember at the medical inspection he was revealed to have an enormously long penis hanging down to his knees. He should occupy himself with that, and leave the good sisters alone.

– Marital service rather than military service, Frederico said.

– And now, the cousin continued: you'll see him always touching men younger than himself, young curates and teachers, to assert his authority over them. It's revolting.

– I remember we were taught touching was a sin, Francesca's husband said: particularly touching yourself. At my last confession, which was thirty years ago or more, I confessed to masturbation. But subsequently I decided it wasn't a sin at all.

He smiled at his wife.

On my other side, Father Michael laid down his fork.

– I was on the phone to Leonora earlier. She told me you'd been badly bitten. Poor you. But the bites don't show at all. I can just see a shadow of one. Here.

He gently touched his finger to my forearm. He stroked it. My belly turned over, somersaulted.

Rosamaria, at a nod from her mother, collected our plates and replaced them with clean ones, went out, came back in with a large platter heaped with *bollito misto*.

Was this conversation a form of priest-baiting? I remembered what Father Michael had said about people being odd around priests. So far none of the women had spoken a word. I decided I ought to join in.

But what could I say about sex? Being a widow, I hadn't had sex for a while. Even when I was a wife I hadn't had nearly enough. I strove to remember. What was sex like? It seemed to be like pain. Once gone forever forgotten. My memories of my sex life with my three husbands blanked out, the surface of my mind smooth as the white napkin spread over my knees. Was that guilt-induced repression, or simple courtesy towards the dead men's right to privacy? For the moment, in any case, all I could think about was the fact that Father Michael's elbow was brushing mine.

– What a delicious joint, I said: I mean these cuts of meat are so beautifully tender.

– The risotto was made with the meat juices from the *bollito*, the elder cousin said, handing me the bowl of *mostarda*: that's why it was so good. And Giovanna is an accomplished cook.

The Contessa smiled at me.

– Take more than that, Aurora. I'm glad you like our food.

Frederico poured us fresh wine. Red, this time.

– He's a sort of pederast, really, the Bishop, Francesca said: you should see him sniffing the little ones making their First Holy Communion. It's not the smell of sanctity he loves. It's the smell of pre-pubescent girls and boys.

– Men are odd sometimes, Contessa Pagan said: I remember when I was pregnant with Frederico, and my husband, may his soul rest in peace, was feeling very anxious, he couldn't cope with it. He rushed out, up into the woods, and dug furiously for the bones of bears. Then he donated the bones to the Museum. They've never been displayed yet, have they, Frederico?

Frederico looked worried, suddenly.

– They must be down in the basement somewhere. There are boxes and boxes down there I haven't sorted through yet.

Rosamaria served us with green salad scattered with blue borage flowers, and with cheese. Then we ate figs. Ah, now I could think of something to say.

– Colette distinguished four colours of figs, I began: blue, brown, pink and yellow.

Francesca, obviously keen to take up the literary challenge, interrupted me.

– And figs come into D. H. Lawrence somewhere, don't they? Into one of his poems. I love English poetry. I read a lot of it at university.

– Figs are sexy, Rosamaria said: they look like cunts.

Her mother raised her eyebrows. Everybody laughed, except for the doctor. He drummed his fingers on the tablecloth. His wife sent him a patient look. Calm down, she's just a child, she's just showing off.

– I love sex, Frederico said, tipping back his glass of golden dessert wine: but women don't want to have sex with me. It's really sad. Women don't fall in love with me. It's because I like them and understand them so well. They tell me that I am a feminist really and no mystery.

Oh, Frederico, I thought to myself: why pretend you're not gay? Why d'you have to hide it? Surely by now your mother must have guessed. It's so obvious.

– That's just what they say to me, too, Father Michael exclaimed.

We were all silent.

– I'm talking of before I became a priest, of course, he added.

– We'll have our coffee outside, shall we? Contessa Pagan said.

We strolled on the terrace, looking out at the tall, bulky shapes of the magnolias. The scent of stocks and honey-suckle rose up into the warm darkness, the dry rustle of oleander. Frederico vanished down the steps into the garden, switched on a floodlit fountain. Its long plume lifted up very suddenly, making us all cry out with delight.

– I like your canister, I said to Francesca: oddly enough I've got one just like it.

– Mine comes from Milan, she said: my mother brought it back for me as a present. I use it as an evening handbag. It holds everything I need.

– Carrying that canister, Michael said to her: you look just like Mary Magdalene. Holding her pot of costly ointment with which to anoint the Lord's feet.

Did he tell every woman he met that she looked like Mary Magdalene? Next he'd be comparing her to the woman in the Bellini painting. Surely if he was such an expert on art history he ought to have other pictorial references at his fingertips? Then, looking at those fingertips, and imagining them stroking mine, I relented.

– Not so costly as all that, Francesca said: it used to hold *amaretti*. Though it does smell nicely of almonds. I wonder what the Magdalene's ointment smelled of?

– Probably myrrh, Michael said: to symbolise her coming anointment of Christ's body in the tomb. The one motif pre-figures the other. Like Eve prefiguring the Virgin, and Adam prefiguring the Saviour. It's called typology. The Gospels are full of it.

– God planned it like that? Rosamaria asked: it seems so neat. Was it like a miracle?

– Stories are written after the event, Frederico explained: so you can arrange them as you want, give them whatever significance you want. That's the point of a story. It's a pattern that you make when you tell it afterwards.

– You mean the Gospel isn't true? Rosamaria asked.

– No, Michael said, putting out a hand to ruffle her hair: it's literature.

Rosamaria jerked her head away and scowled.

– Turbulent priest, I murmured.

Michael turned, caught my glance, smiled at me. I smiled back.

– Let's have a little music, Contessa Pagan decreed: Rosamaria, *cara*, will you oblige? Or Frederico?

– Me, me, Rosamaria said: I love playing the piano.

She thundered through the opening movement of the *Moonlight Sonata*. She played much worse than Lucy in *Room with a View*, in fact probably as badly as Lucia in *Lucia Rising*, and I was relieved when, like Mr Bennet admonishing Mary in *Pride and Prejudice*, requesting her to stop delighting us, Frederico led her firmly from the instrument and closed the lid.

– Enough is enough, my darling. We'll have an encore another time.

We emptied our little glasses of grappa.

– Time to go, Francesca said.

We all said our goodbyes.

– Come and see me again soon, dear Aurora, Countess Pagan urged me: I am off to Milan on Sunday afternoon, for the sales on Monday morning, but I'll be back mid-week. Come for supper before you leave.

I was offered a lift into town on the back of Father Michael's motorbike.

– Oh, all right, then, I said: if you insist.

– I brought a spare helmet with me, he explained: just in case.

I tried not to smirk. Frederico waved a final goodbye

from the top of the steps. Then he ran down them and pulled closed the iron gates. The villa vanished.

Michael and I raced away into the night. I put my arms around his waist. First I held him loosely then I hung on tight, my cheek against his leather-clad back. He went fast. When we cornered, I leant over. It was exhilarating.

– I love riding on motorbikes, I shouted into his neck: Tom, my first husband, had one. We rode all over Europe on it.

Tom liked to feel the wind on his face, in his hair. He didn't bother with a crash helmet when I wasn't around. He made a point of being careless, taking risks. Nobody was unbearably surprised when he fell off a balcony in Notting Hill, drunk and stoned, in the middle of the night. Life was for enjoying, for partying, and if sometimes you overdid it and life rose up and smote you, and turned into death, well, that was just too bad. His coffin careened to church on top of a white Cadillac. Tom would have appreciated that.

We scorched to a halt outside the Museum. I dismounted. Michael took the bike by the horns. He wrestled it by the handlebars into a parking spot.

– Like bullfighting, I said: or bull dancing. Like in Mary Renault.

– What?

– Nothing.

Michael padlocked the bike, locked the helmets into a pannier. We hovered. I prepared to say goodnight and plunge into the gloomy Museum. I opened my handbag to find my keys. Michael put his hand on my arm as a deep, melodious cry rose up into the night.

– What's that singing? Let's go and see.

We strolled into the Piazza. The moon shed milky golden light on the high roofs of the palaces. Strings of fairy lights, at first floor level, looped all the buildings together. People thronged the outside terraces of the *caffes* and the two outdoor restaurants, dawdling over their coffee and wine. Beside the Basilica, seated in a circle on iron chairs, a group of country men in hairy green coats sang a folksong in loud, joyful, harmony. We paused to listen. I couldn't understand the dialect words. Everyone around the twenty-strong choir continued smiling and chattering but the singers concentrated, utterly serious, intent only on the music pouring from their throats, mixing their voices together in sweet counterpoint, as though they were alone just with one another. Both their singing and their devotion made us silent in admiration. At the end, along with everyone else, we applauded. The men began another song.

I looked around for Maude and Father Kenneth but couldn't see them. Perhaps, overcome by watching Padre Pio's mystical powers demonstrated on film, they were exhausted, and already tucked up asleep in the Tre Marie round the corner.

– Such a lovely night, Michael said: pity to go to bed. You're not tired yet, are you? Let's go for a walk down by the river.

We wandered through the side streets, part of a milling crowd. Gradually I realised that all of us had formed into a procession, heading in the same direction. In the distance I could hear a band playing. Trumpet, violin, accordion.

– Did you notice how anxious Frederico looked at one point tonight? Michael asked: after dinner I asked him about it and he told me he's very worried about a recent theft at the Museum.

He took my arm. His touch so delighted me that I could not pay too much attention to his words.

– He didn't say a word about it to me, I said: perhaps he thought it would make me nervous, staying there, if I thought that burglars were about.

– He doesn't want it to get out, Michael said: it could cost him his job, he thinks, if it becomes known that security is so lax. Somehow, the burglars got in past the night watchmen, and managed to de-activate the alarm system.

– Sounds a sophisticated job, I said: I hope they didn't take anything too precious.

I wasn't listening properly, too preoccupied by feeling the bare flesh of Michael's arm against mine and listening to the music. Much louder now. A foxtrot.

We turned the corner and entered a little piazza, edged with shops, boasting a church at one end and a covered well at the other. A large wooden dais, set up in the space in the centre, was packed with circling couples all going the same way, like decorous traffic round a roundabout. The three-piece band sat to one side. On the other, a makeshift bar served plastic glasses of beer and wine.

The music seized my feet and jiggled them. It twitched my hips. I longed to hit the dance floor. More precisely, I longed to dance with Michael. I stared at my feet so that he wouldn't see the craving in my face.

– Come on, Michael said: let's dance.

– I can't, I said: I don't know how.

Sister Immaculata at convent school had attempted to get us to master the waltz, the quickstep and the foxtrot. She showed us the steps, twiddling neatly to and fro, embracing the air, while we copied her and giggled. One by one we were pressed into her starched embrace and led about the floor of the gym while Sister Winifred thumped the piano. Sister Immac's white guimpe stuck out in points. Convinced it was her bosom that was pricking mine, overcome with embarrassment, I tripped over her black nunly shoes. Sister released me from the class and set me to extra Latin instead. After that, when I danced at parties, I danced by myself. The definition of dancing in the seventies: you danced alone, showing off, in a sort of orgy of self-gratification. You didn't have to know any steps: you just thrust and twisted your pelvis and hips. Later on, in the early eighties, when friends got me dancing to soul music, they shook their heads over my inability to learn the simplest steps, move my feet rather than throw my shoulders about. All my life I'd longed to lose myself in a samba, stomp in a tango, jive expertly with a partner. Forget it. Now I was much too old to learn any sort of dancing at all.

– I'll teach you, Michael said: it's easy.

I hate people who say that. It makes me feel more of a clumping fool than ever, when I don't get it, when I fail. I can't bear feeling so inadequate. I would rather not try at all. Nonetheless, I mounted the dais with him and edged into the crowd. The band switched to a waltz.

I clasped Michael's hand, stared at his shoulder. We began to move. I bumped into him. I trod on his feet. I could feel myself going red with mortification. Young and middle-aged couples whirled to and fro in front of us, all keeping perfect time and looking cheerfully contemptuous as they steered competently by. Old people, clasping each other sweetly, trotted past unsmiling and serious. A red-haired man in a trilby steered a plump woman in a magnificent blue gown and curly blonde wig. Two little girls pirouetted and pranced. Everyone could do it except me.

– Sorry, I said: let's stop. I'm hopeless. I told you so.

I sounded as peevish as Harriet Vane in *Have His Carcase*. Like Harriet's swain Lord Peter Wimsey, Michael showed himself able to cope.

– Aurora, he said: you could be a really good dancer, but you've got just one problem. You're trying to lead. But the idea is to let the man lead. We can't both of us do it. Let me, and then you'll see how well we get on.

We moved more easily. Progress of a sort. At least, with him dancing forwards and me dancing back, we were now both waltzing in the same direction. But I was having to concentrate too hard. I couldn't remember which foot did what.

– Come closer, Michael said: to be led, you've got to feel me leading you.

He pulled me into his arms. I flinched, startled. This was like one of my dreams. He was very muscled. His arms twirled me about as though I were a piece of string, and his chest was hard. I was pressed against it. My heart was thundering. He must have felt it.

– Come on now, Aurora, Michael said: enjoy yourself. Don't dance in that namby-pamby fashion. Put some passion into it.

He clasped me even closer in his arms. We waltzed neatly and extremely quickly, doing spins and turns. He was right. It was easy. Borne along by his strength, all I had to do was yield, follow. It was blissful.

Now, suddenly, I did remember sex. Not the sex I'd had so much as the sex I wanted. Dancing like this: sometimes how I wanted sex to be. An active lover, I liked to give pleasure. One by one my husbands turned into the passive recipient who lay back and yielded, the one who got carried away, the one who could take the so-called feminine part. They liked it so much that they wouldn't swap and let me have a go at being given to and done to. Of course men loved being the woman in bed, because in daily life it was forbidden to them. But sometimes women loved being the woman too. Ideally it was a balance and you took turns. Tonight it was my turn to be passive, to be held and twisted and spun and swept away, and oh, I loved it.

We sat and drank a beer and got our breath back. I described to Michael my perceptions of dancing and sex. He smiled and nodded. I suppose I'd passed seamlessly into drunkenness, because my speech now became far too free.

– You'd be wonderful to go to bed with, I told him: I just know it. I can't tell you how much I fancy you. It's such a pity you're a priest. I fancy you so much and you're completely unattainable.

He coughed. He glanced into his beer glass, then at me. His face became impassive. He rested his chin on one hand and bent his dark blue gaze in my direction.

– Aurora, he said: fancying someone, for a woman, that is, simply means becoming possessed by the animus. He's a symbolic figure. He helps you to reach out, cross over into your future. He's there, glimmering through the mists. But then he vanishes, because you've arrived. He isn't real and that's the point. You're talking about a figure in your imagination.

– It does sound a bit incorporeal, I said.

I hiccupped. I became possessed by ineffable sadness.

– You're really keen on Jung, aren't you? I said.

He looked surprised.

– Yes. Didn't I tell you about my current project? I was sure I'd mentioned it. I'm working on a synthesis of Jungian and Marxist thought. That's what my paper tomorrow is about. The Visitation as an emblem of Jung embracing and being embraced by Marx. Speaking of which—

– I know, I said: you want to re-read your paper before you go to bed. Check your footnotes, that sort of thing.

Cecil had done a lot of that. Sat up so late checking his footnotes, very often, that I'd fallen asleep long before he slid in next to me under the sheets. But it was my fault, wasn't it? I'd married him. I'd made my bed and I had to lie on it. And so on and so on.

– I've drunk too much, I said: sorry.

– I'm going to walk you back to the Museum, Aurora, Michael said: and then we'll bid each other a fond and decorous goodnight, and then I'll see you, I hope, at the *convegno* dinner tomorrow evening. You are coming?

We got up from our table and made our way across the little piazza. If I concentrated, I was able to walk without wobbling. People glanced up and watched us go. Flushed and serious, they looked as though they'd be partying until dawn. Was it the Ascension they were celebrating? Or just one more Friday night? I had no idea. But I ought to know. A *festa* was nearly always to do with the Church calendar. I'd been a Catholic once. I could ask Michael. But I didn't want to talk to him about religion. I didn't want to remember his true calling: sworn to celibacy; a priest.

He took my arm. He bent his head towards mine. Tang of Eau Sauvage.

– So you are coming, then? he asked.

What a soft, deep voice he had. Like dark chocolate. When he wanted. Part of me thought he was putting it on. Part of me melted.

– Most certainly, I said: I'm in charge of the special effects.

– What special effects? Michael asked.

– It's a secret, I said.

– Jung once said everybody should have a secret, Michael replied.

He slid his arm around my waist and squeezed. That was unfair. My insides churned riotously. Sweetness fizzed upwards from the base of my belly to my mouth.

– Go on, he murmured: tell me.

Given that he wasn't supposed to go around hugging women, and presumably hadn't had much practice, he knew exactly where to put his hands and how much pressure to exert. I yielded, as I had been longing to do all evening. Also, proud of my prowess up a ladder with hammer and nails, I couldn't resist boasting a little about the spectacle that Leonora and I had prepared for the delectation of the *convegno* delegates. I shouldn't have done that, of course. But I was drunk, and in love, so how was I to know I was giving Michael the wrong idea?

Chapter Five

Next morning, emerging, as usual, from the back entrance
of the Museum, I decided to try a different *caffe* for my
breakfast cappuccino. Somewhere packed and noisy, where
I could forget all about my dream of the previous night:
Father Michael seizing me, pushing me onto the bed,
throwing my legs behind my ears and then licking my
cunt until I came. Accordingly, I walked around to the
front of the palazzo. I found Paolo there, brushing down
the ornate façade of the building with a long-handled
broom, valeting it as lovingly as an old-fashioned wife
might smooth down her husband's jacket before kissing
him goodbye and packing him off to the office.

I had behaved like that once with Cecil, during that
year when we rented a flat in Padenza so that Cecil could
study Balladio's drawings of rulers and set squares. I had
ironed his shirts, had his lunch ready on the table when he
returned at mid-day from the archive, waited for him to
finish talking to beautiful architectural students and come
home late to dinner, watched in silence at parties when he
slipped away with other women and did not reappear for

hours. I had lived for five years in the shadow of scholarship, trotting after Cecil into art historical receptions, listening at dinners to conversations about architectural measurements that I could not join in, sorting out his lecture notes, filing his slides. But then, just before the opening of a conference on Sansovino in Venice, Cecil had fallen out of a hotel window into the Grand Canal and so that was that. It reminded me of what happened to George Eliot's young husband on their honeymoon, only he did not drown and Cecil did. Unfortunately my scholarly husband couldn't swim.

Paolo lifted his broom in greeting and sang out in his husky voice.

– *Buon giorno, Signora.*

– *Buon giorno a lei.*

He carried on dusting as I hovered.

– Everything all right, *Signora?*

– There is just one thing, I said: the water supply up there flows very slowly, just a trickle really, and I can't take a shower. I don't like to bother *Dottor'* Pagan, because he's been so kind, lending me the flat, but in this hot weather it is really hard not to have a proper wash.

– I'll take a look, Paolo promised: and I'll speak to Giovanna as well. She will know what to do.

Reaching the end of the street and turning the corner, I found myself in a different city, the Piazza transformed into a camp, a collection of tents, the entire space taken over by canvas roofs which floated and fluttered like the sails of boats at sea. The market, which must have set up in the early morning, long before I was awake, formed a labyrinth of narrow paths packed with shoppers. I saw much flailing of elbows as people rummaged for bargains, pushing up and down between the striped blue and white awnings that guarded the stalls from the heat. The air rang with cries and shouts, with conversation. I forgot about needing coffee and rushed in.

The stalls closed around me and swallowed me up. Clothes, handbags, bras and petticoats and underpants, embroidered tablecloths and lace curtains, shoes and belts: everything for the body and the bedroom and the sitting-room. At the far end the wares became kitchen-oriented: meat mincers, mousetraps, wooden spoons, rolling-pins for pasta, stone jars, plastic pegs. Tea-towels folded into neat squares; checked and striped and spotted and plain. The juxtaposition of different patterns, jazzy and intense, reminded me of paintings by Vuillard and Matisse. I bought several of these pretty cloths, all in blue and white. I loved tea-towels. Cecil had thought it the sign of a bour-geois, inferior and narcissistic mind, to notice the design of what one dried up with. But I had thought that if you spent time in kitchens, washing up, mopping dry, why not choose your tea-towels to please yourself, give yourself delight each time you used them? Cecil was a scholar of solid walls, I of flimsy fabrics. *Chacun à son goût.*

Round the corner in Piazza delle Erbe, the fruit and vegetable sellers offered trays of produce, wet with drops of

water, in air scented with melons and apricots and tomatoes. I bought a bunch of fat blue grapes and ate them as
I wandered up and down. I selected some more new
clothes: a pair of brown linen trousers, some low-necked
white T-shirts, a set of underwear in white lace, and two
flimsy viscose dresses, one eau de nil and one pale pink.
Everything, as Clara had promised, cost very little.

I spent a cheerful hour buzzing about like a bluebottle,
inspecting the cheese and delicatessen stalls, alighting here
and there, as the whim took me, to get inspiration for re-
stocking my shop. The stallholders, hooking me exactly as
spiders trap flies, commanded me to try their wares. I
sniffed pungent and aromatic olive oil, tasted salami, nib-
bled fragments of sharp, salty cheese. All local produce.
Fresh. Just one sort of oil, two sorts of salami. Nothing
fancy or pretentious. No designer foods in sight. I bought
a packet of *bigoli*, and nearly bought a rock of dried cod so
that I could test-drive the recipe for *baccala* I had cut out
of the airline magazine on the flight over. I wasn't sure
Frederico's kitchenette was up to *baccala*, so I left the cod
behind and went into the nearby *tabaccheria* instead to
buy some postcards.

I had dawdled away the entire morning when, returning
from Piazza delle Erbe through the throng of shoppers to
Piazza dei Signori, I spotted a bright blue suit and a trilby
hat ahead of me. Edmund. He carried a bulging green plastic bag in one hand. I followed him down an alleyway
between stacks of canvas boots and a display of stretchy

sofa covers. He performed a zigzag dance, obviously as mesmerised as I by the sunlight gleaming on the fanned arrangements of net curtains, the deep shadow under the awnings themselves, the dazzle of stripes as you moved in and out of darkness and light. Now he began turning back and forth between racks of flat caps and the array of stiff net petticoats and pink corsets on the underwear stall opposite.

Sooner or later we would have to acknowledge each other's existence. I stepped up to him.

– Hello, Edmund.

He jumped and turned round.

– Dawn.

His face gleamed pink. I felt hot, too. I wished I'd brought a hat.

– Maude's here too, I said: did you know?

He glanced at a tray of men's striped shirts. He pursed his lips.

– Maude's not very missable. It would be difficult to avoid seeing her. I met her yesterday, in fact. She told me you were here too and I told her I hadn't seen you yet. We move in different circles, don't we?

– I'm more missable than Maude, I said: I just wondered whether you minded her knowing you're here. Whether you hadn't wanted some time by yourself.

I put out a hand and fingered one of the frilly petticoats, which hung so close to us that their beribboned edges brushed our faces. They swung all round us with a shushing sound.

– We've discovered, Edmund said: that we're staying in the same hotel. We're in the Tre Marie. Absolutely wonderful place. The best in town.

He gripped my arm and propelled me away from the flounces and furbelows.

– Come along. We mustn't be late. I'm having lunch with Maude and Kenneth at the Gran' Caffe. You'd better come too.

– But I hadn't planned on spending time with Maude today, I protested.

Edmund stuck out his lower lip. Just so had Cecil pouted when I walked barefoot on the floor, forgot to wash my hands before lunch, dropped my clothes at night on the same chair as his.

– Maude will be very hurt, Edmund said: if you don't. Don't be so unkind, Aurora. Maude is the best and sweetest of women and deserves every courtesy.

Today Kenneth sported a cream polyester dogcollar, an olive green safari suit, brown open sandals, grey socks. On the other side of him my stepmother smouldered in ruched emerald green with matching high-heeled mules. A pink suede bag, its open top gathered and drawn together with metallic pink ribbons, presumably bought in Rome, jutted from her lap. She patted the chair next to her and Edmund sat down. To anyone else she would have complained that the colours of their outfits clashed: blue and green must never be seen. But to Edmund she gave an approving nod and a smile.

– Yes, very well indeed, she said to me before I'd spoken a word: fine.

That was her telephone manner, answering your opening question before you'd asked it.

– And Padre Pio? I asked: good film?

– Maude wasn't feeling so good, Kenneth said: so I went on my own. Wonderful, so it was, Dora. A complete inspiration.

– I needed a rest, Maude said: all the excitement in Rome nearly wore me out. But then later I felt much better. And today I'm so happy because we can all be together. Poor Edmund had got picked up by two terrible women. You needed our protection, dear, didn't you?

She beamed at him.

– You saw them off, did you? I asked: I thought you might.

– Just a couple of tourists, Edmund said: they were leaving this morning, in any case.

Maude waved an arm and hailed the waiter in English.

– Come along, there. Look sharp.

I immediately lowered my gaze, not wanting to catch the waiter's eye, his look of contempt. I sat down, picked up the menu and studied it.

Maude had chosen a table set in the shade of the awning. We sat well away from the hubbub of the market, which bobbed and swayed at the far end of the terrace like a ship at anchor, pulling against the restraining chain. A merchant vessel, a trader on a leash, desperate to be off.

The *caffe* floated, marooned, becalmed, but the market rode the waves, dipped up and down, mobile. Soon it would vanish. I remembered the flat in Venice Cecil had rented, at the top of the tall, thin house in the *calle* leading from the vaporetto landing at Santa Maria del Giglio on the Grand Canal. From our attic window I used to look out at the frieze of roofs and watch the masts of ships gliding past, the ships themselves invisible, the masts tall as the spires of churches, as though Venetian churches were magical and free, could slip their moorings and travel off to whatever destination they chose.

I had forgotten to bring my sunglasses. The midday light bounced off whiteness: the fringed parasol above us, the plastic chairs and paper tablecloth, the pavement, the urns of flowers. Against all this crackle of white Maude's red-gold hair burned like a torch. Too much brightness; I felt tired.

We caught up on each other's news. Rather like the newspapers back at home, we offered our own version of events tailored to suit the political and moral views of the company. All of us, of course, were having the most wonderful time.

– Poor you, Maude said to me: in such a cramped little place. Whereas we've been so fortunate. Our rooms are really super.

– Have you seen Father Michael this morning? I asked.

– He's back in the hotel, rewriting his lecture, Edmund said: in the light of some recent revelation or other. Some overnight inspiration that apparently came to him. I must say, I always, when giving conference papers myself, got them finished as far in advance as possible. That's the professional, the scholarly way. It doesn't do, this constantly changing one's mind. One ought to develop one's thesis, and stick to it.

– The dear boy, he does work so hard, Maude said: but so kind too. You know he's got us tickets for the opening dinner tonight? He just rang up your friend Leonora and fixed it. He doesn't want us to be left out of anything.

She gazed reproachfully at a pigeon pecking up crumbs nearby and flapped her menu at it to frighten it off.

– My goodness, Kenneth said: shan't we be grand.

– So we mustn't eat too much now, Maude said: just something very light.

The waiter paused by our table. We scanned our menus.

– That's all they serve down here, anyway, I said: light things. The restaurant's upstairs, on the floor above the café. Here it's just bar snacks.

– I don't really like Italian food, Maude said: in England you get far too much of it, huge platefuls of noodles you can't possibly eat, and out here the plates are too small and there's hardly any sauce at all, just a dollop on top. I must say I'm rather disappointed.

– Oh, Kenneth said: but we didn't come in order to feed our faces, now, did we? We haven't even begun telling Doris and Edmund yet about all the wondrous holy sights we've seen.

143

I ordered for all of us, so that I wouldn't have to listen to my companions issuing loud commands in English while the waiter shrugged. I settled on *tramentini*; safe and inoffensive. I liked the way the *tramentini* were piled up on lace-edged paper doyleys in the display case to tempt you when you came in: so dainty, each small square sandwich cut apart into two crustless triangles, transfixed by a cocktail stick, the middles turned towards the outside so that you could see the fillings facing you. Little bulges of slivers of artichoke hearts, and prawns, and mayonnaise.

– We mustn't have wine, Maude said: not in this heat. It'll be too much.

– In that case a beer, Edmund said: for you too, Kenneth, I'm sure.

How firmly he spoke. Maude glanced at him with respect. I ordered a bottle of mineral water, two beers, and a white wine spritzer.

– I think Michael's making a novena, as well, Kenneth said: for a friend who's lost her faith. He wouldn't come out with me to the film last night. I think he was praying.

The *tramentini* arrived. A neat pyramid of plump white cushions topped with a parsley sprig. Maude picked one up and shook her head.

– What's this?

She tore open the little sandwich, scraped out the mayonnaise, replaced the lid of bread. Then she handed it to me.

– There you are, darling.

– Who's that glamorous woman over there? Edmund asked: trying to attract our attention.

I put down my *tramentino* and pushed back my chair.

– Back in a second. I've just seen someone I know.

Paolo's wife Giovanna was hovering, with her back to the market, at the far end of the terrace, looking intently in my direction, clearly wanting me to notice her. Today she wore a sleeveless scarlet frock, a white rose hair-grip, and red shoes with white polka dots. I went over to her.

– *Buon giorno, Signora. Come sta?*

– *Signora* Aurora, she said, shaking my hand: I have telephoned to *Dottor'* Pagan about the problem with the water, and he is very sorry, and he is sending a workman to fix it this afternoon. So tonight you will be all right. You can have a proper shower.

I began to thank her. She raised a hand to stop me.

– You know I work as housekeeper at the Tre Marie, don't you? I thought, if you don't mind coming with me now, you could have a shower there. Paolo said you'd had no shower for three days. He is so sorry. But he didn't know.

It had not occurred to me previously but now it did: I could ask Maude to let me use the shower in her room. The obvious solution. Instantly I decided against it.

– Oh, *Signora*, I said: that's so kind of you.

– It's the staff lunch break at the moment, Giovanna said: so if we went now, I could show you an empty room to use, with a bathroom. You could be in and out while the *padrona*'s having her rest, without her ever knowing.

I waved to Maude, Kenneth and Edmund, pointing at Giovanna and then at myself, inventing a semaphore of gestures to indicate that I was unexpectedly called away on urgent business that did not permit of a second's delay. Just like Colonel Brandon being summoned away from Lady Middleton's breakfast table in *Sense and Sensibility*. I followed my deliverer through the piazza, now rapidly emptying of people. The awnings, wound around their poles, were coming down as the stalls packed up. Men dismantled the metal skeletons, tossed the ringing aluminium poles onto barrows. Orange wrappers, bits of spoilt fruit, vegetable stalks, littered the ground. Municipal dustcarts waited nearby.

Giovanna turned into a dark, deserted alleyway, halted in front of a door in a blank façade.

– Here's the hotel.

– It doesn't look much like a hotel, I said: the entrance is so discreet.

– This is the back way in, Giovanna said: and in fact it used to be a brothel, many years ago. But the Commune converted it and so now it's turned into a hotel.

She fished in her pocket for a key.

– Come. I'll take you to the room.

The door scraped to behind us. We curled up three flights of narrow uncarpeted stairs, through a baize door

146

and into a gloomy corridor lit by dim yellow lights in cut-glass shades. The colours of the floor gave it a congealed look: marble chips, speckled purple and pink and white, exactly like salami flecked with fat, just as Frederico had said. A shuttered grey metal box indicated the presence of a lift.

Giovanna unlocked a door.

– In here. It's been cleaned this morning, and no one's due to come until later this afternoon. The last of the guests for the *convegno*. Please help yourself to the soap and towels and shampoo. I'll pop in later and replace them. Take as long as you like. No one will disturb you.

– I'll clean up after myself, I said: I don't want you to have to do it.

– Here's the key, Giovanna said: lock yourself in, and then when you're finished leave the room unlocked, just leave the key behind you in the door, and you can let yourself out downstairs. The street door opens from the inside. *Ciao*.

She smiled, waved, vanished.

I moved into the stuffy darkness. The room's drawn shutters kept the air and light at bay, but the heat had got in centuries ago and now it came up to me like a heavy animal and pressed its moist fur against me. Sweat started up on my forehead and temples and flowed down the sides of my cheeks. I kicked off my shoes. The uncarpeted marble floor felt clammy against my bare soles. Jam-coloured, raw liver-coloured: a particularly bloody slice of meat. A large bed, covered with a red velvet counterpane, protruded from the centre of one wall, flanked by a little night table bearing a lamp. Three armchairs eyed each other stiffly. A tall walnut veneer wardrobe supervised from a corner. Beside it, a door led into a bathroom tiled in pale orange.

Hot water gushed from the tap when I turned it on. Scorning a mere shower, I filled the bath and added the hotel's scented salts. They and the shampoo came, I saw from the brown paper label on the blue glass bottles, from the convent apothecary shop. A little packet of convent soap sat nearby, outfitted, elegantly as the nuns' habits, in pleated brown tissue paper and white string, sealed with a blob of wax and smelling of carnations.

I dropped my clothes onto the floor. I basked in warm water and lemony foam and lathered myself with spicy soap. I washed myself several times just for the pleasure of it, rinsing my hair until it squeaked. I anointed myself with vanilla and orange body lotion. Then I put on my new underwear, and my new eau de nil frock, rapidly cleaned the bath, bundled my discarded garments into my carrier bag, and crept out into the corridor.

Nothing and nobody stirred in the dimness. A faint smell of meat ragu hung in the air: I sniffed peppercorns and tomatoes and onions, a dash of cinnamon and clove. Everybody must be asleep after their good lunch. I made for the back stairs as softly as I could, the handles of my carrier bag over my arm.

Footsteps. I halted. Giovanna, a white apron tied over her red frock, appeared out of the gloom at the far end of the marble salami strip, bearing a tray. White napkin covering a dish, green neck of bottle perspiring in ice-bucket, wine glass. A silky-looking white duster dangled by one corner from her apron pocket.

– Lovely bath, I called: thank you so much.

A hoarse voice from the floor below cried out.

– *Arrivo, arrivo. Aspetta mi. Ma dove sei?*

The lift mechanism creaked, whirred. Giovanna, cocking an ear, looked alarmed.

– The *padrona* is on her way to inspect the room you were using, before the guest arrives, she hissed: she never trusts the chambermaids to clean properly. She mustn't see you up here. She'll know you're not a guest. I'll be in such trouble.

– Where are you going with that tray? I asked.

– Number thirty-three, at the end there. He left a note last night saying he wanted his lunch sent up. The waiters are fast asleep so I thought I'd bring it.

I seized it from her.

– I'll take it. She won't see me if I'm in someone's room, and then I'll slip out while she's inside checking the other one.

– Quick, quick, Giovanna whispered.

She gave me a little push. I went clumsily with my burden back down the corridor, my carrier bag swinging and bumping against my skirts.

Giovanna clicked her tongue behind me. I turned. She chased after me.

– I forgot. It'll be locked. Here. I'll let you in.

I slid through the door of number thirty-three. Giovanna pulled it shut behind me.

A sword of brilliant light slashed the gloom. The shutters had been pulled to, and the window left open a crack. The cool air of night-time had not been completely chased away. I turned, balancing the tray on one hip, holding it with one hand, and felt with my fingers for the wheel of the lock. I double-bolted the door behind me, just in case the *padrona* arrived in hot pursuit.

My nostrils caught a trace of Eau Sauvage. Gradually my eyes made out the bed. I inched towards it. I bumped into something and swore.

A sleepy murmur answered me.

His voice. My stomach turned over. My cunt began to thump.

– Your lunch, sir, I whispered.

He didn't stir. So I put the tray down on the table blocking my path and took off my clothes. I laid them on top of his, on the armchair. His yellow paisley socks gleamed in the half-dark, flung down on top of his white shirt.

Later that afternoon I tested the plumbing in Frederico's little bathroom. I stood in the hip-bath turned shower and let soft tepid streams tumble over me. I dressed for the *convegno* dinner in my indigo linen outfit. I hoped there wouldn't be too much speechifying before we ate. Hunger gripped me, because I had missed lunch.

My mobile beeped.

– Aurora, Frederico said: is the water all right now? I am so sorry. I never thought to check it.

– Perfect, I said: really wet.

– Would you like to see round the Museum? And then shall we go up to Leonora's together? May I escort you? We could have an *aperitivo* first. That would be nice, would-n't it?

Frederico showed me the Museum in double-quick time. He whirled me from room to room, from gallery to gallery. It was like being carried away on a breeze. A brisk zephyr of a breeze in an exquisitely tailored grey silk suit and with winged feet. Groups of tourists and of school-children stared at us as we flew past.

We circled the first floor at top speed. Annunciations, Nativities, Crucifixions.

– Lots of minor seventeenth-century religious paint-ings, he said: rather dull, mostly, so I've had them hung all together. Now let's go and look at the good stuff. We've got a little bit of nearly everything.

We wafted up the wide stairs. He indicated the periods covered by the galleries as we sped through. Roman glass-ware in pale jewel colours. Terracotta pots with snaky rims. Painted majolica ware. Etruscan tomb sculpture: a reclining man, lean and long legged, with a wide thin mouth, smiling. Fifteenth-century fabulous landscapes with people dancing. Sixteenth-century classical myths and allegories. Naked men and women entwined and laughing. Drinking wine and eating fruits and going hunting and killing each other. Cupids and grotesque beasts, gods and goddesses, nymphs and satyrs and bacchantes, fabulous monsters and sea-serpents and flying fish, all rose up to greet us as we rushed towards them, embraced us, and then fell away again in our wake. In this Museum I had no sense of history or of death because everything seemed alive. It was alive. The art had made the stone and canvas and paint spring awake and dance and sing.

– Oh, no more time, Frederico cried: let's have our *aperitivo* in my office and then we must go. It's through here.

We ran past a double door, high and closed. A sign said 'Work in progress – keep out'. Hammers, coils of wire, lengths of plasterboard lay about. The air swirled thick with dust.

– That's the new textiles gallery, Frederico called over his shoulder: I hope we're going to open on schedule. There's still a lot of work to do. We only started hanging the exhibition two days ago. I'll show it to you as soon as it's finished.

Around the corner we entered a marble-framed doorway. Darkness. Frederico fumbled for a light switch, found it, pressed it down.

– This used to be part of the archive, but I'm turning it into my office because it's such a nice place to work in.

Shelves stuffed with boxes tied up with black ribbon and labelled with roman numerals took up one wall. Vellum-bound and calf-bound books occupied the second. Across the remaining two walls stretched a fresco of a banqueting scene, more opulent than The Last Supper in Leonora's refectory, and featuring not Jesus and the Disciples but Bacchus and his friends, half-naked gods and well-dressed sinners, in lace collars and slashed satin sleeves, reclining on couches. High above them, around the cornice, pranced a troop of kilted Amazons, arrows at the ready, each hunter with a single breast exposed, long hair flowing from under plumed helmet, little gilded boots on her elegant feet. An antique desk in one corner, piled high, shed papers, drifts of photographs, memo pads, sketches. A work station carried a bank of machines: computer, printer, fax machine and telephones. Reams of printout scrolled across the floor, over heaps of books and journals.

– It's a little chaotic, Frederico said: with the exhibition coming up there's so much extra paperwork. And I'm rather untidy at the best of times. My assistants are in despair, because it means I am often losing things.

He opened a small fridge perched on a filing cabinet.

– Is prosecco all right? Chin-chin. And try one of these little savoury biscuits. They're delicious.

We walked about, looking at the frescoes and the books. Frederico told me of his dream the night before.

– All about Danae. I think I was Danae. But I was the shower of gold as well.

We left the Museum along with the last dawdlers. The guard was one I hadn't met so far. He nodded at us, jangling his keys.

– Goodnight, Maurizio, Frederico said: alarms all set? No burglars tonight let's hope.

He stood still for a moment, sighing. Then he pulled out a packet of MS and lit cigarettes for both of us.

– Remember how all the feminists used to smoke these? Now we all think we should be giving up.

We descended the shallow flight of steps leading from the portico into the street, turned, and strolled across the Piazza.

– I hadn't told you about the burglars because you have your own problems to deal with, Frederico said: your own griefs. And you're very English, aren't you, Aurora. You don't talk about your feelings. Stiff upper lip and all that. So I didn't want to obtrude my concerns.

– Do tell me if you'd like to, I said.

– I've made up my mind I've got to let the police and the insurance people know, Frederico said: obviously I must. And take the rap for carelessness. But I'm going to wait until after the exhibition opens. It's just possible the police would want to close the Museum down while they investigate, and that would ruin our timing. All the galleries who've lent us artefacts for the show would have to have them returned. We'd have to cancel the exhibition altogether. No, what bothers me most is that I feel I'm dealing with some kind of maniac. Someone who breaks in and despoils some things and steals others.

– Steals what? Despoils what? I asked.

– Steals seventeenth-century gowns from the textile gallery. Despoils wall hangings and bed curtains waiting to go into the display cases. Cuts out squares from them.

Out of the corner of my eye I suddenly saw bright colours flicker like warning flags.

– Oh dear, I said.

– I knew you'd sympathise, Frederico said.

I turned my head to check. At the far end of the Piazza, inside the archway marking the foot of the convent steps, just about to begin their ascent, a group of people stood and dithered. Three of them, joggers in skimpy vests, one purple and two black, danced up and down on the spot. As I gazed, the athletes braced themselves, hit the first flight of steps at a sprint, turned the corner under the arcade and vanished from view. The four other pedestrians, more smartly dressed, followed them. How could I not recognise them? Plodding up after the joggers, in a blaze of emerald ruching, sapphire suiting and ecclesiastical grey swathing, went Maude, Kenneth, Michael and Edmund.

– We're not in a rush, are we? I asked.

We leaned against the base of one of the lion statues, finishing our cigarettes.

– Thanks, Aurora, Frederico said: you've got such a nice way of listening. So quiet and sensitive.

– Thank you for telling me in the first place, I said: I'm sorry I'm so bad at telling you things in return. I've recently discovered I'm an extrovert. I prefer to act rather than to reflect.

– Criminals are extroverts, Frederico said with a sigh: they act all right. They break in and destroy things. They don't worry about how other people feel.

We began our climb up into the radiant sky. Heaven wrapped itself around us like a cloak, warm and milky blue, transforming us into the tiny people in a painting of Our Lady of Mercy who shelter under the blue fall of the Madonna's sleeves, her outstretched arms.

– It's still rather hot, Frederico said: let's go gently. We'll stop for a cigarette half-way, shall we, have a little rest.

Around the corner, on the first zigzag, we found the others. The jogger in the purple vest flopped on the sill of the arcade, his back against a column, gasping. A tendril of flowering jasmine, hanging down from the branch above, had caught in his curly black hair. Red-cheeked, wreathed in glossy green leaves and white flowers, he looked like Bacchus in the fresco in Frederico's office. Maude and her entourage, making courtly gestures of concern and respect, hovered at a polite distance, a couple of steps below him.

Michael, glancing back, spotted us, caught my eye, and nodded coolly. My insides did a somersault. A foolish grin I could not stop erupted and spread across my face. That afternoon when I had crept into his room he had thought

I was his lunch arriving and had stayed, lolling like a lord, half-asleep. He lay on his back, arms outflung, head turned aside into the pillow. Gently I turned down the sheet so that I could look at him. The light fell through the gap between the shutters onto his body. I gazed, enraptured. Then I drew the sheet back up a little way and wriggled in underneath it. I could feel his drowsy heat and smell his smell, aftershave and sweat mixed. I touched him tenderly. I stroked his face. I climbed into his embrace before he could wake up. His arms closed round me and he murmured pleased words. Goodness knew who he thought it was he was kissing. Perhaps he believed I was the Lord Jesus, come to him in a vision. By the time he had discovered my identity, it was too late.

– Heavens, said Frederico in my ear: it's the Bishop.

The two joggers in grey vests were, I now realised, priests. Like their boss, they had abandoned their dog-collars, which hung half out of their trouser pockets, and carried their shirts and suit jackets over their arms.

Frederico and I halted. We stood four steps beneath Maude and company and stared tactfully at the view while the Bishop tried to compose himself, panting, wiping his red, sweaty face on the sleeve of his jacket, putting his hands on his knees, dropping his head and taking deep breaths. He was a fat man and, of course, as I knew from my own experience, it is very difficult to ascend steep hill-sides rapidly when you are overweight. It is best not to be over-optimistic about getting up fast.

– Oh, it's you, Maude cried.

She darted down to my side and I introduced her to Frederico. She flung out her hand for him to kiss, then whispered into my ear. A Maudish whisper, carrying and clear.

– His Eminence has been telling us about a charismatic retreat he attended recently. It convinced him to abandon the pomp and props to which he'd become accustomed and completely renew his life. So, although he'd thought of paying his inaugural visit by helicopter, he decided instead to run.

– Isn't that grand and holy, Deirdre? Kenneth said, joining us: though of course one mustn't overdo it.

The Bishop sat up again. He leaned back and addressed Kenneth and Michael, attendant archangels in shimmering polyester, in a peevish tone. He seemed to be including Frederico and myself, also, in his remarks. He obviously needed a big congregation to complain to.

– I decided to arrive early, to have a few words alone with the Abbess, so I came ahead. But I had not expected the ascent to be this steep.

His face was as purple as his ecclesiastical vest. Italian bishops, I noted, did not wear crimplene but silk. The two aides' vests were cotton. Beautifully cut.

– Is there no other way up? moaned the Bishop: I've changed my mind. We really ought, in this day and age, to be able to get there by car. Making us climb all these steps is ridiculous, in this weather especially.

He squeezed his sopping handkerchief between his hands. He frowned at it.

– Have I got another one? Who laid out my clothes for me tonight?

He fished in his pocket. He pulled out a second handkerchief. It was made of black lace.

– Oh, oh, murmured Frederico.

The priestly aides' cheeks blushed pink as cherubs' bottoms.

– You must have picked them up by mistake, they said to one another.

I recognised my knickers. I must have left them behind in the Tre Marie bathroom. So this was the guest the *padrona* was fussing over.

The Bishop turned redder than ever. I inspected a Judas tree that was managing to grow out of a crack between boulders in the hillside.

Edmund leaped up the steps and reached forwards.

– Here. Let me.

Deftly he palmed the knickers, pulled out his own handkerchief and handed it to the Bishop. A large, clean square of green crepe. The Bishop grunted. He wiped his face. Edmund slipped the knickers into his pocket. The two aides scowled. Then Kenneth took the Bishop's arm on one side and Edmund on the other. He shook them off.

– No.

He re-positioned himself just behind them, his arms outstretched, his hands resting on the backs of their necks.

– So.

– Come along everybody, chirruped Maude.

She skipped ahead, skinny and fit as a little mountain goat.

I fished out my mobile and murmured into it.

– Bishop alert. Bishop alert. He's on his way. He's coming early on purpose. I think he wants to take you by surprise.

Just below the last turn in the marble staircase we stopped again. The Bishop and his two acolytes donned their shirts, jackets and dog-collars. The Bishop took out a gold signet ring from his pocket and put it on. We fell into line for the final stretch: men of the cloth first, male civilian next, women at the rear.

At the top of the three hundred steps, framed by a wisteria-tangled arch, a trinity of nuns waited to welcome us. Leonora, very commanding and upright, stood flanked by the Mistress of Postulants and the Mistress of Novices, two lively old generals whose black eyes shone like apple pips in their wrinkled brown faces. The nuns' costume this evening was impressively ugly and modern: calf-length black polyester overall, very badly cut, shapeless black acrylic cardigan, thick flat sandals over woollen stockings, white alice band holding black nylon veil. Plastic rosaries dangled at their sides from plastic belts. Their hands hid out of sight in that classic gesture of modesty I remembered from convent school, crossed then folded into their baggy sleeves. As soon as we were within hand-kissing distance, they put on reverent faces: eyes cast down, smiles, faint and sweet, allowed to touch the edges of mouths.

Leonora stepped forward, bent the knee, and kissed the jewelled ring jutting from the Bishop's outstretched hand. The two other nuns followed suit. Slow, obviously arthritic, they lowered themselves to kneel before the cross, sweaty man.

I looked at Michael, who had turned back to stand next to me. He frowned.

– I can't bear those elderly nuns having to genuflect like that. It's disgraceful. Our Lord would never have permitted such a thing.

Catching my eye, he looked away. Earlier that day I'd done him reverence, I'd kneeled to kiss his cock, I'd kissed it over and over, but of course that was different.

– You're so radical, Father, Maude said: but you see, they like doing it.

– Blessed humility, it's called. You get a blessing when you kiss a Bishop's hand, Father Kenneth reminded us: as I'm sure we do for climbing all those steps like the good pilgrims that we are!

– If Leonora thinks she's fooled the Bishop with that little display, Frederico murmured in my ear: she's got another think coming. He's not that stupid.

Leonora waved us towards the door in the high wall.

– Aurora, will you and the others join our sisters for a drink in the cloister? You know the way, don't you? Please go ahead. The Bishop and my two colleagues and I shall walk more slowly than you, so that we can have a little conversation as we go along. I cannot relinquish this opportunity of a private audience with His Eminence. Such a privilege to be afforded time alone with him!

The two priestly aides, thus dismissed, joined our inferior group. We processed along the avenue under the cypresses. I recognised the terracotta pots holding miniature lemon trees that surrounded the cloister well: they had been moved, and now lined both sides of the gravel. They looked very festive, the dark green leaves glossy and shining, the lemons glowing like lamps. A new arrangement of small bay trees in tubs indicated the end of the path.

Up the graceful stone stairs, in under the portico, through the big double doors we went, into the vestibule. Here we paused. Maude marched across the tiled floor, heels rapping, beckoned to an attendant novice and asked for the cloakroom. The men drifted after her. From behind a column Rosamaria bounded out to greet Frederico and myself. She danced up and down, her clenched fists punching the air. Her black curls sprang around her head. She wore baggy combats, a white T-shirt, an olive army jacket.

– You here? I said: surely this isn't your kind of thing? Oughtn't you to be out clubbing or taking drugs?

– Don't be silly, Aurora, she replied, sounding very like Leonora: you're thinking in clichés. As a matter of fact I'm writing this up for my cultural studies project at school.

162

She came closer and opened her clenched fists. Frederico lit a cigarette, his face a bland mask. Rosamaria held out her hands to me, palms up, displaying the red marks at the centre of each.

– What d'you think the Bishop will make of that?

– Lipstick? I asked.

– Oh Aurora, please.

I peered closer. Wounds. Blood-encrusted scars at the edges, open, gaping holes at the centre, fresh blood seeping from them. I knew that troubled teenaged girls these days had a tendency to cut themselves, but this was a new one on me.

– Stigmata, Rosamaria said: impressive, huh?

– I didn't notice any wounds on your hands before, I said: surely you'd have to wear bandages? And surely stigmata appear on Fridays, because of Good Friday, don't they?

Rosamaria clicked her tongue.

– Aurora. This is the modern world. God doesn't want them to interfere with my homework during the week. They appear on Saturdays. I have to have the weekend off.

She darted away. I saw her approach Kenneth and Edmund, on the other side of the entrance hall, who were holding Maude's handbag and parasol. Where was Michael? He had disappeared.

Frederico touched my arm.

– Stick-ons, I'm afraid. She gets them from the joke-shop on the boulevard leading to the station. I took her to the funfair there the other night and afterwards we went across the road for ice cream and discovered the shop. Rosamaria's completely hooked.

He lit another cigarette and gave it to me.

– Come on. Let's go and find that drink.

The nuns had turned the cloisters into a temporary restaurant roofed by the blue evening sky. Trestle tables, draped with lengths of white brocade banded with gold embroidery, surrounded the square grassy space edged by the arching columns. The well in the centre of the cloister garth had been transformed into a bar, strung with fairy lights, presided over by a young woman in starched white shirt and black tails, black jeans and black cowboy boots.

– The tablecloths are all antique altar cloths from the seventeenth century, Frederico said: the convent's got quite a collection. Leonora considers she's got no use for them in the chapel, since Mass can't be said there any more, so she's brought them out for this party. Not such a good idea tonight, perhaps, with the Bishop here. A little bit too provocative.

Gleaming mousse burnished the barmaid's blonde ·crewcut. Her sparkly blue bow-tie matched her blue eyes.

– Hi, Sister Clara, I said.

She greeted us with swift kisses, then wound up the bucket from the well, dipped in a ladle, splashed pink cocktail into flared glasses, handed us one each.

– Aurora, it's so nice to see you. Hope you like this. My own recipe. How is your food research going? What are you doing tomorrow? Would you like to have lunch with me out in the country? My parents and I are going to see my grandmother and I thought you might enjoy coming too.

– I'd love to, I said: thank you.

Frederico took a sip of his drink.

– Convent Bellinis. Not bad.

The rosy nectar, prosecco and peach juice and something else I couldn't identify, slid, cold and potent, over my tongue. My second glass of fizz tonight. I felt drunk already. The effects of the bottle of Pinot Grigio I had shared with Michael earlier this afternoon had not worn off either, nor the dope I'd fished out of my handbag and rolled a joint with, before getting ready to come out. How useful that gold canister had been. Years since I'd smuggled dope but I hadn't forgotten the arts of dissimulation, surprise and double bluff. This time I'd hidden the dope inside a polythene sachet under a thick layer of Hugh's ashes. Just as I'd predicted, the Customs Officer had thought my trick too obvious to be true. I could not help feeling a tiny bit smug.

People were crowding in. Frederico pointed out conference delegates, senators, art historians of every European nationality. Some Americans, too. I recognised several of the male art historians, the ones who had dominated every *convegno* in years gone by. Presumably they were really famous now. They strode in scowling, and trailed clouds of minders. They sported exquisite haircuts and looked poured into their suits. They posed themselves in corners, like statues on terraces, and grimaced, cold and unapproachable. At any moment an admirer might dart up and try to take a bite. These cheeky fish had to be frozen off at fifty paces. The middling famous art historians were having a more cheerful time, chatting together in one big crowd. The un-famous ones, the young, hovered on the edges of the throng, observing everyone. Lots more women in these last two groups than there had been twenty years ago.

– I'll have to go and do my duty, Frederico said: talk to some people. I promised Leonora to help take care of her guests. The nuns are acting as waitresses but she needs an extra host. Will you be all right?

– Sure, I said.

I wandered over to my English compatriots, who stood in a tight little knot in a corner of the cloister, sipping their Bellinis. I felt tipsy, and stoned, and very relaxed. The pomander-cloister, with its pierced walls, held and released the perfume of convent pot-pourri: box and dust and hot stone. The warm night air stroked my bare arms. Bats flew past, very close, skimming our elbows.

– The programme is dinner first, Edmund was announcing: not too formal, hardly any speeches, and then there's some kind of short theatrical performance outside here in the cloister.

– Yes, I know, I said: I helped Leonora set things up. Just you wait and see!

How foolish I sounded. Maude glanced warningly at the half-empty glass in my hand. Don't overdo it, dear.

– The *convegno* proper will take place in the chapel, Edmund went on: with Michael's talk to kick it off.

Michael had read me several pages of his Introduction earlier in the day. He planned to compare dialectical materialism with projective identification. Could Christ, the carpenter, represent both Animus and Worker? I had distracted him by dripping white wine into his navel and then licking it up. If you won't lie still, he'd threatened: I'll have to make you.

– Would you have liked to give one of the talks, Edmund? I asked.

– Certainly not. I can't respect a *convegno* such as this. In my day there was no such thing as cultural studies and I must say I think we were the better for it. Scholarship was scholarship. Connoisseurship had its place. Art history was art history. Not all muddled up with feminism and structuralism and psychoanalysis and I don't know what else.

– Personally, I like the Impressionists, Maude said: but they don't seem to have any round here. Though of course the Impressionists did not tend to paint religious subjects, did they, Kenneth?

– Oh, it's all Bellini, Bellini, Bellini in the Veneto, he said.

– The man who invented this cocktail? It's very nice, Maude said: but rather strong and I should think terribly fattening. Better not have another, Dawn, or you'll get over-excited. And alcohol does pile on the empty calories.

The bell clanged. The signal for dinner. Leonora, the Mistress of Postulants and the Mistress of Novices, reappeared with Michael, the Bishop, and the two priestly aides. The three senior nuns had changed their clothes, donning magpie black and white to match the postulant-waitresses flying to and fro with charged trays: winged white caps, black dresses, white cuffs, white aprons, black lace stockings and flat black shoes.

Our little party of English visitors tucked ourselves into place at the end of a long table. We all sat facing inwards into the garth. Leonora, spotting me, darted up.

– I could kill that bloody man, she hissed.

– What's he gone and done? I asked.

– I'll tell you later. I could murder him.

– Oh Leonora, don't do anything rash.

The high table dominated the side of the cloister backing onto the chapel, facing the doorway to the *brolo* beyond. The dignitaries sat down, the Bishop in the exact centre, flanked by Leonora on one side and Michael on the other. Above him, unnoticed by anyone, it seemed, except myself, ran the wire on which the dove would travel in to signal the start of the conference and the moment of the Annunciation. The Bishop was so placed that he sat directly underneath the firework-stuffed figure of the Virgin Mary. She clutched an Old Testament in her hands, inside which, two days ago, following Leonora's instructions, I had concealed a Catherine wheel.

Frederico arrived, carrying an extra chair.

– Here comes my admirer, Maude beamed: isn't he sweet?

She sounded like an echo of Mrs Gibson in Elizabeth Gaskell's *Wives and Daughters*. Mrs Gibson, too, I reflected, had been a stepmother.

– So that I can sit here with you, Frederico said: is that all right?

Maude patted the tablecloth.

– Come here. Sit by me, dear.

He parked himself at the end of the table, next to me. The Bishop intoned a lengthy Grace.

The novices and postulants ran about, serving us. *Pappardelle* with peas, broad beans and mint, garlic-studded chunks of roast lamb with rosemary-strewn fried potato dice, strawberries sprinkled with red wine and sugar, almond cakes.

Once all the plates were cleared away and we were left with our thimbles of grappa, the Bishop heaved himself up. He was still red in the face, shiny with sweat, and breathing heavily. Leonora half-closed her eyes. Her mouth looked zipped shut. Michael seemed restless, constantly glancing about.

– What's that he's saying? Maude asked: I can't understand a single word.

I translated. Like Anne Elliott in *Persuasion*, at the concert in Bath, I gave just the gist of the speech, for who can explain the words of an Italian sermon?

If one did not know that the Bishop was newly converted to temperance, one would be tempted to say he was drunk. So tactless was he; so zealous. He began by praising the charismatic renewal now underway in Italy, with its stress on simplicity. He denounced superstition, which had no place in the modern Church. He denounced relics, in particular the relics newly brought back to this convent, and unwisely, he might say blasphemously, over-venerated by the Abbess and her credulous sisters. Although the convent was doing a great job attracting tourists, it needed to ensure it did not decline into some sort of theme park for sentimental reactionaries. Nuns these days did not need their own chapels but should attend Mass and the sacraments in their parish churches where they could be seen to be part of the congregation. They ought to be out and about in the world doing good works, properly involved in the apostolic labour of the diocese, properly supervised by their diocesan superiors. Of course, the Bishop concluded, he was no enemy of correct and socially useful intellectual endeavour and therefore he was delighted to declare this *convegno* formally open.

Leonora smiled, her lips together; a long, curving smile. She smoothed her white gloves.

She looked towards the open door, the darkness beyond, and raised her hand, pointing upwards with her index finger just as angels do when they've got something important to say and need urgently to catch your attention. This was the signal for Sister Clara, outside, to mount her stepladder and light the bunch of sparklers on the dove's tail.

A sudden lively fizzing made us all look up.

The dove, blazing and sparkling, shot in through the doorway and streamed on wings of fire along the wire above our heads.

Leonora stood up and produced a pistol from her pocket. My pistol.

The dove crashed into the Virgin, who burst into flames with a roar, ribbons of fire whirling about her ears, her Old Testament flaring as it spun and blazed between her crackling hands.

Leonora fired.

People screamed.

– Oh dear, Frederico said: I am afraid the Bishop has exploded.

The prelate's face turned a deeper shade of crimson as he spread his arms wide, jerked up and back, then slumped, face down, onto the tablecloth.

Every door around the cloister burst open. Policemen raced in, their guns raised. Michael leapt to his feet.

– Everybody stay where you are, he yelled: this is a police raid. Sister Leonora, you're under arrest.

CHAPTER SIX

The following morning I accompanied Maude, Kenneth and Edmund to the airport in Venice. If I saw them onto the plane for London then I would know they had really left. They could proceed thence on to Walsingham or other shrines if they wanted, but I wouldn't have to be involved.

Edmund wore his safari suit to travel and carried two bulging bags.

– That's a beautiful new suitcase you've got there, Kenneth exclaimed: and very heavy it looks, too.

– I bought a lot of art history books, Edmund replied: and a few clothes. Italian clothes are so well cut.

Kenneth had resumed England-coloured grey-black crimplene and lugged a carrier bag full of pamphlets on Padre Pio. Maude's Chanel-style orange jersey suit exactly matched her hair.

– I shan't be sorry to get back to Greenhill and a decent cup of tea, she declared: and then we've got the Middlesex Latin American semi-finals to look forward to, haven't we, Edmund?

– That is so, dear lady, he replied: and some hours of practice, also.

We travelled to Venice by train, getting on the *locale* by mistake. It jolted to a halt at every tiny pink-washed station en route, making us slither to and fro on the hot, shiny seats, then crept on again like a dormouse through the rustling maize.

– I still can't believe it, Kenneth said, sighing: Michael had such a lovely priestly presence. The way he glided about the sanctuary in his alb, you'd think he'd been a priest in his cradle. Of course, I never thought to ask for references when he volunteered to help out. Why would I?

– He might have been a paedophile, I said: out to corrupt the Girl Guides.

– No, Daisy, Kenneth said: he came to me for confession, his first day. I would have known. Not that I would have said anything, of course.

– He'd have been lying, though, wouldn't he? I said.

– Dawn, dear, Maude said: now do remember who you're speaking to.

– I imagine he would look very nice in a cassock, Edmund said: he's got the height for it. The legs. Not everybody could carry that off.

– Let's look on the bright side, Maude said: you never know, it could be the way he'll discover his vocation. Perhaps he'll leave the police and train. Become a missionary. He's good at rounding people up.

– Dispersing them, you mean, I said: he had the whole *convegno* cancelled, for heaven's sake.

– Health and safety grounds, Maude said: which was quite proper. You can't sit and listen to a lecture when people are creeping around letting off fireworks and shooting pistols.

Arriving much later than planned, we took a water taxi to the airport. We skimmed across the lagoon, bumping and bouncing. We hurried into the terminal. Glaring from the check-in desk, the BA clerk, in her ugly, badly cut uniform, waved us forwards urgently.

– Quick. They're boarding. I think you'll just make it.

She frowned at Edmund's two large cases.

– You're way over. The extra weight is going to cost you a fair bit. I'm not sure we've got time to sort this out. Not if you want to catch your plane.

I stepped forwards and lifted his second case, the fatter and newer one, off the belt.

– I'll bring this home for you, then you won't have to pay excess baggage. I've only got one small bag. I'll give this to Maude to give to you when I see her next week.

– Hurry! cried the clerk.

We said our swift goodbyes.

– Don't forget, darling, Maude said to me: go easy on the pasta and the olive oil.

Father Kenneth pressed a holy picture of the Madonna of Medjugorje into my hand.

– I forgive you everything, Delia. Be sure I'll pray for you.

– You must come for supper sometime, Edmund said.

I waved the fraught pilgrims into Departures and watched through the glass wall as they skipped through Passport Control. Then they disappeared from view.

When I got back to Padenza I took Edmund's suitcase to my room at the Museum. Then I went to the police station to find out what was happening to Leonora. The duty officer explained they were letting her go without charging her. She had to stay down in the cells while they completed the paperwork. This might take a little time. I could sit and wait for her in Reception if I wanted to.

I settled down with my copy of *Middlemarch*. Half an hour later, Leonora appeared, and we walked out into the sunshine.

– I haven't spent a night in jail since the seventies, she remarked: I must say conditions have not improved.

– I had a call from Sister Clara on my mobile just now, I told her: the Bishop's in hospital, apparently going on nicely. He's out of intensive care and into a private room. He did indeed have a heart attack but is well on the way to recovery.

– I hope the rooms in hospital are more comfortable than the cells in jail, Leonora said: I shall go and visit the Bishop sometime soon, in a spirit of forgiveness and charity. It's important to show him I don't consider the disarray last night to be totally his fault. I must say, *cara*, I think that policeman friend of yours rather over-reacted.

The dinner had broken up in noise and confusion. Sister Clara had phoned for a flying ambulance to come and collect the unconscious Bishop. Leonora had been hustled away. People stampeded for the exits, only to find them guarded by armed police, apparently summoned by Michael who for some reason had suspected an assassination plot on somebody's part. Eventually, once it became clear that nobody had in fact been murdered, and having given our names and addresses, we were allowed to go. We left the nuns behind in the cloister garth, clearing up, and streamed out into the night. A police helicopter, bristling like a vast, malevolent mosquito, was parked on the gravel beyond the portico. Above it the black sky glittered with stars.

Sister Clara pursued me and grabbed my arm.

– Poor Sister Leonora. They didn't even give her time to pick up her cigarettes.

– I'm sure she'll be all right, I said: she's not easily frightened. Don't worry.

The city dignitaries hustled past. Frederico waved to me and hurried after Rosamaria and Francesca. The *convegno* delegates vanished towards the retreat block, doubtless to smoke, drink grappa and discuss the events of the evening. I decided to accompany the little contingent from the Tre Marie back into town and see them safely to their door. While they hung about under the portico, putting on their coats, I went back inside the convent in search of Michael. I discovered him stamping about the cloister, shining his torch into the darkness behind columns, flashing a beam of light at the bosses on the vaulted ceiling. He didn't seem to have found anything, which perhaps accounted for his frown.

— You've made a terrible mistake letting Leonora be arrested, I told him: she never intended to shoot the Bishop. She only wanted to give him a fright.

— Luckily for Sister Leonora, Michael said: she forgot to load her gun. Nonetheless she's in trouble.

He pulled up his trousers at the knee and crouched to inspect a dark corner. His socks were black, with white spots.

I slid closer to him. He stood up.

— Well, I'm off now, I murmured: perhaps I'll see you later at the hotel?

His face became cold and distant.

— Certainly not. There is work for me to do here.

He looked through me, as though I were a very clean window.

— The local police searched your room in the Museum earlier today, Aurora. That gold canister you carry. You must think I'm terribly stupid not to have guessed what was in it. The police couldn't find it in your room, but that's because you carry it everywhere in your handbag. Come on, open up.

His hand shot out and grabbed my handbag. He extracted the canister and unscrewed the lid. The gold container held a powder compact, a spectacles case, a folded hand-kerchief, a tiny green glass bottle of perfume.

– Oh dear, I said: I seemed to have picked up Francesca's evening bag by mistake.

This was just like the miracle that happened to St Elizabeth of Hungary. Forbidden by her mean husband to take bread to the poor, she nonetheless filled her apron with crusts. Caught, commanded to open her apron and reveal its contents, she let fall a shower of roses.

Michael scowled.

– I thought you fancied me, I said: was that a mistake too?

– I'm a detective, Michael said: detectives have to have sex with suspects. It's part of the job. Don't go getting ideas. Just remember, Aurora, I'm hot on the trail.

– I can't think what you mean, I said.

I took the gold pot back from him. I opened Francesca's spectacles case, took the glasses out and tried them on. The effect was acute. Everything came sharply into focus. Now I could see that Michael was just a bit too handsome.

He brushed past me and strode away to join the group of Italian policemen standing about, hands on holsters, in the centre of the cloister garth, supervising the novices who were loading glasses onto trays, folding tablecloths and righting upturned chairs. I found my stepmother and her companions and walked with them down into the city. Negotiating the slippery marble steps in the dark, we had to concentrate in order not to miss our footing. Conversation seemed inappropriate. Kenneth began chanting the Rosary, to raise our spirits and implore heavenly protection for our dangerous descent, and kept it up even when we had reached the Piazza. So I said my goodnights under a hail of Our Fathers and escaped to the Museum.

The guards were not visible. Doubtless they were making their rounds. I let myself in through the back door, as usual, de-activated the alarm for the mezzanine floor while I got upstairs, and then set it again.

Having undressed and lain down in bed I found I could not sleep. My heart pumped and thundered. Too much drink. Too much excitement. Heat washed through me. The burning tip of the mosquito spiral, glowing red, reminded me of bites and itchiness. I threw back the top sheet but still tossed to and fro. I got up and drank some water, lay down again and tried my usual cure for insomnia, reciting a list of deli suppliers to whom I owed money. That usually did the trick.

Then I heard a noise.

Footsteps, going very quietly, but distinctly, up the staircase just outside my door.

I told myself it must be Paolo, making his rounds. But what if it were the burglar? Or the ghost?

One of the advantages of the extrovert personality, I remembered Michael saying during a pause in our love-making earlier in the day, was that extroverts tended not to feel fear. It had been a helpful and reassuring comment given that he had just produced a black leather gag, a whip and a pair of handcuffs from under the pillow.

– I am an extrovert, I reminded myself: and I do not believe in ghosts.

I set forth to catch the burglar. I donned my blue silk dressing-gown, and armed myself, for lack of a better weapon, with Francesca's gold canister. Failing my mother's pistol, which had been confiscated by the police, how I wished I had brought my father's truncheon with me. But, not imagining for a moment I might need it, I had left it behind in London. I thought I could probably stun the burglar with the canister if I concentrated and if he had his back to me and stood still for long enough while I crept up on him. If he attacked me, I would employ the self-defence moves learned in the Girl Guides all those years ago. Their successful utilisation depended on the attacker being deep in thought when you approached him and not fighting back while you tossed him over your shoulder. I took my mobile as well, just in case. I slipped it into the pocket of my dressing-gown.

I glided upstairs to the *piano nobile*. The glass doors to the Department of Textiles were open. A dim light from a source I could not identify showed me that the posts looped with red cords, barring the exhibition entrance, had been moved aside. I tiptoed into the cardboard vestibule of the opening section of the exhibition. Placards of explanation in big text loomed over me, interspersed with grainy blown-up images from old books. I felt like a bookworm nibbling her way through an opening chapter. Ringleted ladies in stomachers and ruffs gestured at gentlemen in slashed doublets and lace collars. They spoke to each other in seventeenth-century type-faces. The story had begun, all right, but its language slithered past my ears: incomprehensible.

I moved forwards as slowly and gently as possible into the main gallery, on tiptoe, arms out for balance. Ghosts walked like this in cartoons. My bare feet made no sound on the polished parquet floor. Shapes seemed two-dimensional. The drawn-down blinds, pale blanks, held back the moonlight. A pile of carpenter's tools formed a jagged dark mound to my right. Perhaps the workmen were simply carrying on through the night to make sure that the exhibition would open in time. Perhaps I needn't have bothered getting up at all. But now I'd reached this point, I felt I had to find out what was going on.

I had entered a vast wardrobe. A closet of disguises. Pastel satin cloaks gleamed as though washed in star-water. The stiff bodices and full skirts of long dresses, suspended in the air on strings, glimmered in the darkness. They swung at me, resident spectres greeting a visiting phantom. I hovered behind a case of seventeenth-century pantaloons, trying to decide what to do next. Listening to the silence, its creaks and whisperings, I got used to it. I edged forwards. Peeping around a display of laced busks, I fancied I saw a pencil of torchlight at the far end. A shoe-sole squeaked. He was coming this way.

I hesitated, then drew out my mobile. Of course. I must phone Frederico. As the Director, responsible for security and answerable to the state authorities, he ought to be informed. He could ring for the police while I tied up the burglar with the cord of my dressing-gown. How long would it take him to arrive? I wasn't sure. And supposing the burglar were armed? I wasn't ready to die. I hadn't yet made my will. If I died tonight nobody would know where I wanted my ashes to be scattered.

I fumbled with the phone. Luckily I'd programmed Frederico's mobile number into the memory three days ago.

He picked up almost immediately.

– Frederico, I whispered.

– Aurora, he whispered back.

– Where are you?

– I'm in the Museum. I'm lying in wait for the burglar.

– What a coincidence, I exclaimed: so am I.

Something rustled close by. My insides convulsed. My knees felt like loose string. Perhaps I wasn't an extrovert after all.

– Hang on, I whispered into the phone: I'm just going to perform a citizen's arrest. Shan't be a minute.

Hands came from behind and grabbed my waist. I jumped and cried out. I whirled round and threw myself at the intruder. He wouldn't stay still. I couldn't perform any of my self-defence moves. Unexpectedly strong, he had my arms pinned to my sides.

Then I smelled the fragrance of juniper.

– I'm here, Frederico said: it's me. I've got you.

The burglar, if there had been one, had fled. Maurizio and Paolo, summoned, rather late, by the noise, went back downstairs to continue their night patrol. We retired to Frederico's office for a restorative shot of grappa.

— I'm afraid tonight's intruder was just you and me, Frederico said: nothing's been taken, anyway.

Once installed in the comfort and protection of the large armchair in the ex-archive, I abandoned my weapons, dropping gold canister and mobile phone onto the rug at my feet, and gave way to the shock produced by the events of the night. I disgraced myself, abandoning all pretence at a stiff upper lip and instead bursting into tears. Frederico passed me his handkerchief and I wept into it. Like Mr Darcy watching Elizabeth cry in *Pride and Prejudice*, he observed me in a compassionate silence. I found myself telling him, through my sobs, all about my hopeless passion for Michael, its brief-lived consummation and climax, its disastrous aftermath. I skipped over the details of Michael's attempt to interest me in bondage, feeling sure that wasn't something someone with Frederico's exquisite sensibilities would want to hear.

— No normal man has ever loved me, I cried: I only attract weirdos and art historians and VAT inspectors and fake priests. And now I've discovered that I don't even attract them.

— Most men are weirdos, Frederico said: you just have to get used to it. And I did have my suspicions about

Michael. His socks were too elegant. And of course his shoes, once you looked at them properly, were pure policeman.

– There's something terribly wrong with me, I wept: I'm not a real woman. I'm not like other women. I'm a freak.

– Oh, if that's all, Frederico said: don't be so hard on yourself, Aurora.

He took the empty grappa glass from my hand and looked around for a clear surface on which to place it among the welter of books and papers. His glance took in Francesca's gold canister lying on the rug at my feet. The lid had fallen off and the contents had tumbled out. He picked up the tiny green glass perfume bottle.

– Here. Have a sniff of this. One of Clara's potions from the convent shop. It's called Essence of Woman. Francesca always takes it with her to parties. Perfect for those moments of stress when you become overcome by anxiety and self-doubt.

He waved the bottle under my nose.

– Me, I think grappa does the job just as well.

– I'm sorry, I gulped: I know men hate women crying.

– Oh Aurora, Frederico said: Englishmen perhaps. But I am Italian, don't forget. I am used to displays of strong emotion.

He patted my shoulder.

– Cry away as much as you want. I am going to do a spot of tidying up. And then I am going to write a list of things I must do tomorrow morning.

I blubbed and snorted while he pottered about behind me, opening and shutting filing drawers, shuffling papers. My tears died down. Stopped. Then I yawned. I felt quite wrung out. My eyes felt sore. Should I check my appearance? I wondered if Francesca's powder compact contained a mirror. No, I couldn't face it. Elizabeth Bennet probably looked lovely after weeping. I was sure I didn't.

– I must look terrible, I said.

– No, you don't. You look a bit wet, that's all. I'll find you another handkerchief, and you can dry your face.

He bent down, picked up the canister again, and pulled out a folded square of white material. He shook it out. Antique silk, freshly frayed at the edges, as though recently cut. I'd seen another one very like it recently, but where?

– Aha, Frederico said: I shall have to ask my sister about this tomorrow. I mean this morning. Look, it's dawn. We should get some sleep. I've got to get up early to go and talk to the police. And now I realise I must go and see Francesca as well. And then I have to cook lunch for my mother before she leaves for Milan.

Grey light gleamed at the window and probed my eyelids. I felt very tired. Grief, and excitement, plus not being used to staying up all night.

– Frederico, I said: it's too far for you to drive home now. Why don't you share my bed? I mean yours?

We arranged ourselves in the way that Hugh had shown me on the nights when we were not allowed sex.

– It's called bundling, I explained: it's an old Scottish

custom for courting couples, from the days when they weren't supposed to sleep together but wanted to get close on the long winter evenings.

You put three sheets on the bed. One of you slept between the bottom two and the other between the top two, so that there was one between you, a separating skin. People in novels used bolsters, or swords, but sheets worked perfectly well. Frederico found a third sheet in a cupboard and we made the bed accordingly.

Frederico butted his head into the pillow. He yawned, and patted my arm. Some men are patters and some aren't. His pats seemed like punctuation marks. A form of italics. Or, possibly, indications of invisible footnotes.

– You patter, I said: the patter of tiny footnotes. Sorry, not original but I can't remember what novel I've pinched it from.

– Stop making terrible jokes and go to sleep, Frederico said: goodnight, dear Aurora.

– Goodnight, I said.

I switched out the bedside lamp.

Frederico whispered in the dark. His warm breath rested on my cheek.

– I'm not infringing some unspoken feminine rule, am I? Are you sure I'm not supposed to pounce on you despite all these sheets? Because, lovely and desirable as you are, *carissima*, I am afraid I am too tired. You're not offended, are you, Aurora?

– Not at all, I said.

I smiled at him even though he couldn't see me smile. Frederico had such a kind heart that he could even pretend not to be gay in order to make me feel not rejected.

– You know, I said, settling myself: you are not a man like other men, Frederico. For example, you've never told me not to be silly. You've never told me to calm down. You've never told me I was crazy. All my husbands always kept telling me that.

– Leonora tells people quite often not to be silly, Frederico pointed out.

– I suppose she has got a strong masculine side, I said.

– Masculine, feminine, who cares? I just like crazy people, Frederico said: that's why I love Leonora. For example, well, she must have told you this, she used to keep samples of her bathwater in bottles, to remind her of particularly beautiful bathtime experiences. She did experiments with her tears too, trying to find out whether tears of joy tasted different from tears of sorrow. I suppose that led, eventually, to her interest in relics.

He yawned.

– Ah. That reminds me. Before I go to sleep I must tell you about my dream last night. I was hearing the Pope say Mass. He wasn't wearing a cope, just a nappy, and at the Consecration he said: this is my piss, and this is my shit, given to you all in remembrance of me. Michael would say that was very Jungian, wouldn't he? In his autobiography Jung talks of dreaming about God doing a big shit.

Michael was the big shit in this instance, I thought.

– Michael wanted to make a synthesis of Marx and Jung, I said: I wonder what the Marxist interpretation of your dream is. There's supposed to be a connection between shit and money, isn't there?

Mentioning Michael's name did not make me burst into tears all over again. That was something. Perhaps the improvement in my morale was to do with Clara's potion. I fell asleep.

Frederico had gone by the time I woke up. He had left me a note scribbled on a packet of cigarettes: I've taken Francesca's canister with me, and I'll bring yours back sometime later today.

Having hurried over to the Tre Marie and collected Maude and company and seen them off to the airport, having collected Leonora from the police station and accompanied her into the centre of town, I dawdled with her as far as the bottom of the convent steps. It was still only eleven o'clock. I needed to collect myself now, and my thoughts.

– What are you going to do next, *cara*? Leonora asked: when is your rendezvous with Clara?

The sun was hot on the back of my neck. Pigeons pecked crumbs from the pavement. Flocks of Padentines, dressed in their smartest Sunday outfits, strolled up and down, chatting. Church bells were ringing, summoning the faithful to Mass, but nobody around me seemed in a hurry to leave the sunshine and light outside. I felt loose, unanchored, as though I might drift off. Leonora looked tired.

– I need some coffee, I said: how about you?

– I'm starving, Leonora said: how about breakfast?

We ate brioches and drank espressos, standing at the bar in the Caffe Elizabetta. I filled her in with details of the night hunt in the Museum. She looked impressively vacant. She knew or suspected something, but she wasn't going to tell me what it was. At least she couldn't have been the burglar. She had an alibi. She'd been in a police cell all night scratching socialist-feminist graffiti on the walls with the sharp edge of the crucifix on her rosary.

– I don't understand how Michael was able to fool you that he was a bona fide cultural historian, I said.

– Oh *cara*, Leonora said: but he was bona fide. Lots of policemen have to moonlight these days, I believe. And many of them are intellectuals. Some of them even write poetry. Look at Adam Dalgliesh.

– What are you going to do about all the *convegno* delegates? I asked: won't they be rather upset at coming all this way for nothing?

The brioches were fat with apricot jam, dusted with almonds and icing sugar. We each took a second.

– Oh, I've already sorted that out, Leonora said: before the police remembered to confiscate my mobile I was able to call Clara from my cell and get her to organise everything. We're going to shift sessions and venues, that's all. The delegates have done their sightseeing this morning, rather than on Monday. We're going to re-convene at the Tre Marie. Meet at one, have a nice lunch, give everyone a chance to recover from all the excitement, and then get cracking at two. We'll slot in a couple of extra evening sessions to ensure we cover everything.

– Except for Michael's talk, I imagine, I said.

Leonora spoke through a mouthful of brioche.

– Of course. That's been cancelled. It's a pity, but there we are. Michael's tied up on police duty all day today, he told Clara when she rang. Apparently something has come up via Interpol that he's got to help with. Now, Clara also told me she's having lunch with you. Please make sure she's back in good time, won't you?

I waved Leonora off up the steps. She raced round the first bend, her back looking very determined. I returned to the Piazza and strolled towards the Museum carpark.

– *Ciao*, Aurora!

Clara, in her white sweatshirt, jangled her car keys. The convent car turned out to be a neat minibus, capable of holding a dozen nuns at least. Bright yellow, it had Brigandines painted along its side in large swirling letters.

– We'll go to the *mercatino* first, Clara said: collect Nonna, and then we'll drive up to the mountains, meet my parents at the restaurant, and eat.

We left Padenza by a back road lined by lime trees whose fallen yellow flowers, like twists of tissue paper, silted up in long drifts in their dappled shade. Through the maize fields we sped, towards the blue hills rising up in the distance.

Clara's grandmother lived in a village in the process of turning into a suburb. New concrete bungalows, decorated with fancy tiles and wrought iron, were wedged in between old farmhouses. The *mercatino* took place in an open shed in a farmyard. A press of women was jostling to get to the front and be served next. They wore clothes straight out of glamour magazines: bright sequinned T-shirts, sparkling earrings, big hair clips, platform sandals. The outfits made them utterly modern, and yet some of their faces, serious, heavy-browed, with straight noses and fine eyes, were exactly the same as those in the Renaissance paintings in the Museum.

The women surged around a counter made of wooden boxes. Three cheerful servers in blue overalls, standing behind this, cracked jokes with their impatient customers, weighed out produce taken from the big open trays of fruit and vegetables laid on the ground. They kept the shoppers sweet with gifts of a plum tossed here, an apricot there. Nothing could be further from the smart aluminium decor of Italian food shops in London. I wondered if I should re-decorate the deli, do nostalgia, go for a 1960s fake-rustic look. Lamps made from straw-covered wine flasks, travel posters, bunches of plastic grapes, a fishing-net or two full of plastic lobsters and glass floats.

We bunched in the doorway, at the back of the crowd.

– There's Nonna, Clara exclaimed.

The small white-haired woman flew out of the throng of customers towards us, smiling. Bright blue eyes, just like Clara's, in a wrinkled brown face. She wore small gold earrings, a sleeveless cotton frock flowered in red and blue, a pink and white striped overall, a pair of wellington boots.

We put the shopping in the minibus and drove Nonna home. Her little house was in a suburban street that had obviously recently been a country lane. Glittering pink and green pavements and sparkling tarmac divided lines of plane trees, plots of vines, big vegetable gardens. Nearby ran the railway.

Nonna showed me around her house, proudly indicating all its mod cons: a big TV, a hi-fi, a dishwasher, washing-machine, large fridge and microwave. Nothing could have been further from an English style magazine's idea of a peasant dwelling. The sitting-room's white tiled floor, and the picture windows, were polished to brilliance. A leather three-piece suite surrounded a coffee-table with a mosaic top. A wrought iron lamp-post sported a pleated shade, holders for magazines, two pots of geraniums. Ornaments trotted along the windowsill: panniered china donkeys bearing tiny baskets of flowers, statuettes of puppies and cats. In between these stood some clever modern copies of old pots. Moulded of some resinous material, these looked remarkably authentic.

– And look at my bathroom, she exulted: hot and cold running water. Everything.

The bathroom tiles, separated by pink grouting, depicted ladies in crinolines and bonnets. The design was a little girl's dream of beauty, cherished all her adult life, unspoilt because kept inside her and never taken out to be tarnished by the air, and now at last allowed to flower into reality.

The bathroom moved me. Italy was certainly having an effect on my emotions. My carapace of extroversion was beginning to crack.

– You sit down, Nonna said: while I go and change.

– Let's go outside, Clara suggested: so that you can see the garden.

I admired the dense ranks of peppers and aubergines, the tomatoes, their vines bending under their weight. The fruits, reddening, were cracked and craggy and smelled of earth. Grapes grew along the edge of the tin roof of a little shed. Rows of salad greens flanked a plantation of courgettes bright with yellow flowers.

Nonna re-emerged, dressed in a white leather catsuit.

– *Avanti*, she cried out.

Clara drove very fast up to the restaurant she had chosen, in the foothills of the mountains. Zigzagging past vineyards, we arrived in a hamlet which consisted of no more than a bus-stop, a telephone box, several houses, and a parking bay jammed tight with cars. We parked by a small chapel and walked down a rutted stony track under a heavy canopy of chestnut trees. It began to rain, very gently. The warm air steamed with drizzle. We hurried around a corner.

– *Ecco lo*, Clara exclaimed.

The place seemed pure 1960s. The vine-hung courtyard, floored with cracked cement, with a shabby bar at one side, a big freezer in one corner and a pinball machine in the other, was set with formica-topped tables, plastic-strung chairs. Under the green ceiling the atmosphere was cool and moist. Through the bead curtain at the far end we went, into the restaurant proper, where Giovanna and Paolo were waiting for us. This was clearly a popular place. The big whitewashed room was packed with families seated at heavy brown tables and chairs. Modern copies of old ones. Everyone in Sunday best, white lace blouses and very clean check shirts. Squalling babies were arrayed in pink or blue frilly frocks and white bootees. Older ones were tottering across the red tiles, watched over by brothers and sisters.

Kisses, welcomes, exclamations done, we sat down.

– Do you want to try smoked horse with lemon? Clara said: would that go down well in north London? Or here's *bigoletti* with squid-ink. I always think it looks just like nuns' jumpers unravelled.

– First of all let's order some wine, Paolo said: the wine here is very good.

A carafe of white wine with a dry sparkle arrived. Clara ordered a lagoon-full of fish: sea-snails and skate and squid. The people on the next table were eating a *fritto misto* of prawns and octopus arranged in a high pyramid on a big platter, surrounded by halved lemons. Pink whiskers and tentacles poked out of the golden crust.

– Fresh as fresh, Clara said to me: they whizz it up from the coast every day.

– This is so nice, Giovanna exclaimed: I'm looking forward to eating a meal I haven't cooked for once.

– You're very busy all week, aren't you? I said to Giovanna: working at the hotel and helping out Frederico at home as well.

– Oh well, Giovanna said: the extra money comes in useful, and I like the family. Rosamaria, for example, is a wonderful child. So full of inventiveness. At the moment she's making patchwork. Something to do with a school project, I think. Some banner or other to go with the show at the Museum. I've been collecting bits of material for her. There was a whole heap of stuff in the Museum, down in the rubbish room, waiting to be thrown away. I gave her some of that.

– Where's the rubbish room? I asked her: I didn't see that on my tour when Frederico took me round.

– The basement, the rubbish room, whatever you call it, she said.

– You've been down into the basement? I asked: forgive me, but wasn't that a breach of security?

Paolo looked defensive. He showed his annoyance by reaching for the packet of breadsticks and jabbing one onto the tablecloth as though it were a knife.

Giovanna shrugged.

– I went down there one day to look for a mop, when I'd come to meet Paolo from work and some schoolchildren had dropped ice cream onto the floor in the entrance hall. Paolo was still busy, so when I took the mop back I thought I'd give the *Dottore* a hand and start doing some tidying up.

– He's so chaotic, Paolo said: he needs someone to help him get organised. He's always losing things and getting behind in his schedule.

– But what a mess, Giovanna said: boxes of broken pots and bones, piles of old dustsheets, pieces of statues, dirty old pictures. I put the worst of the junk on one side, and I brought some of the broken vases home for Paolo to mend.

– It's a real skill, china-mending, Paolo said: you have to make sure not to put on too much glue.

I remembered the line of vases on his mother's windowsill.

– You gave Nonna some of the mended pots?

Nonna nodded. Her white leather catsuit creaked as she leaned forward.

– They look as good as new, mended, she said: as long as you don't get up too close and see the cracks.

– And you gave Rosamaria pieces of old dustsheet? I went on: are you sure that's what they were?

– I know an old sheet when I see one, Giovanna said: they're what I work with all day long. Believe me, these were old. Almost completely worn out. Old bedspreads and things. So I cut some pieces out for Rosamaria. She was very pleased. It's important to recycle things, you know.

Just as our *risotto di mare* arrived my mobile beeped. I'd forgotten to turn it off. I blushed with embarrassment.

– Oh, I'm so sorry. How rude of me. Please forgive me.

Paolo waved a hand.

– Go ahead.

Reception was halfhearted. Leonora's voice, wavering in and out, sounded deep under the sea.

– Sorry to interrupt your lunch, *cara*. But I need Clara back here now. It's nearly two.

– Oh dear, Clara said: I hadn't realised it was so late. Leonora hates unpunctuality.

– We'll take Nonna home, Giovanna said: don't worry. Off you go.

– I'll come back into town with you, I said: give you moral support.

We kissed the others goodbye and instructed them to have second helpings of everything, to make sure our lunches did not go to waste.

Clara sped us back down into town. The roads were clear. All the Padentines were sensibly indoors, eating. Just as well, given Clara's way with corners. It helped, when we were halfway round, to discover nothing coming at us in the other direction.

My mobile rang again.

– How was your lunch? Frederico asked: I cooked priest-stranglers flavoured with spinach. They were excellent. Then we had roast veal and salad. And cold caramelised rice cake.

– Don't talk to me about food, I said: I haven't had any.

– I've tackled my sister, Frederico said: and it turns out that Rosamaria is the culprit. Of some of the thefts, at least. She has promised to confess everything, so as a reward for her information I'm taking her to Luna Park. Would you like to come too? You could be a witness. Shall we meet you there? I've got your canister to give back to you.

I rang Leonora, to explain I would miss the re-convened *convegno* session, but her mobile was switched off.

– I'll tell her for you, Clara said: don't worry. She'll understand.

We entered the somnolent city near the railway station and raced along the wide, tree-lined boulevard leading to the old town.

– I'll ring you later, Clara promised: and tell you how everything goes. What's been happening. Shall I drop you here? There's the funfair, just over there.

They stood waiting for me just inside the entrance. Rosamaria was in combats and a camouflage T-shirt. She looked sulky. Frederico, his hand on her shoulder, was in jeans and a blue shirt. His jeans were perfect.

– I think the big wheel is a suitably dramatic venue, don't you?

He shepherded me into a little boat-shaped carriage, and sat down next to me. Rosamaria insisted on going in a carriage on her own, so that she could feel more scared. We were bolted in by a thick lever that pressed across our laps, but it was easy to imagine falling out as our swinging gondola was swept up into the sky and the park shrank beneath us and we were reduced to trinkets dangling on the charm bracelet of some giant. From behind us Rosamaria called out her story as we soared and plunged up and down, round and round. Her narrative erupted like a serial, in sections, interrupted by screams, bursts of music, gasps.

– I did it for Aunt Leonora. It was a *furta sacra*. She'd told me all about them. I was going to write it up for my cultural studies project at school and then also post everything on the convent website. They needed publicity because they need money. Aunt Leonora needed some relics so I went to the Museum to get her some. The whole point was I had to steal them. I thought I'd get those bones of bears that Grandmother is so fond of talking about. I went down into the basement several times and poked around but I couldn't find them. Then Giovanna found me down there one day and gave me some bits of old cloths she was tearing up for dusters. I made up a story about why I wanted them, and she believed me.

– She's been covering up for you, you mean, I shouted: she could have got into serious trouble. She's been destroying ancient artefacts without realising what she was doing.

– My story was partly true, Rosamaria shouted back above the blaring hurdy-gurdy music: we were cutting up scraps of material for patchwork to make a banner. It was our school project to go with the exhibition. I thought if I couldn't have bones then bits of old sheet would do instead.

– How did you get down into the basement in the first place? Frederico called.

– Giovanna knew how to work the alarm. She helped Paolo change a fuse one day. Your alarm system was so easy to dismantle, Frederico, honestly, Rosamaria screamed back: a child could have done it. I'm afraid I often forget to reset it though.

– Which of course allowed the other burglar to get in, Frederico cried: oh, you wretched child.

We tilted, toppled forwards and plunged down. I yelped. Frederico grabbed my hand.

Up we swooped again. Frederico released me, fished in his jacket pocket, drew out my canister.

– Sorry, I forgot, he said: this is yours.

This would be the perfect moment. Quick. I unscrewed the gold lid and upended the pot as dramatically as I could.

Nothing fell out. It was empty.

The music ceased. We slowed, began our final descent.

– I'm afraid that without her glasses, Francesca's eyesight is very bad, Frederico said: and her imagination over-compensates. She thought, forgive me, seeing all that white powder, that the canister was full of cocaine. Since the police were running about everywhere she got into a panic. So she poured it down the lavatory.

Luckily, I had taken out the sachet of cocaine from underneath the ashes and the packet of dope as soon I had arrived in Padenza. The dope was already gone, but my little cache of coke reposed on a high shelf in Leonora's guestroom bathroom, masquerading as bath-salts. I hadn't told her I'd left it there. I'd planned to surprise her, share it with her on my final night. I thought she might not have had any cocaine for a while.

– Sorry, Hugh, I murmured.

Had they in fact been Hugh's ashes? Or Tom's? Or Cecil's? I couldn't be certain. Things often got mixed up on the deli shelves when I was dusting. I decided I would have to come back to Italy with the other two pots and scatter the ashes of my other two husbands. I would do it properly next time.

Back on the ground we staggered and stumbled, wobbly-kneed.

– My *furta sacra* would have looked so great on the convent website, Rosamaria sighed: I took a video camera in with me, you know. I could have turned my film into something interactive, a kind of mystic magic medieval treasure hunt.

– But they weren't medieval cloths you were stealing, Frederico exclaimed: they were from the seventeenth century.

– Whatever, Rosamaria said: they were old, right?

She pursed her lips at him and shook her head.

– You scholars. These are postmodern times, Uncle

202

Frederico. The past is a ragbag, a dressing-up closet, right? Don't be so pedantic.

She wandered off to search for popcorn. Frederico and I climbed the steep stairs behind the helter-skelter. I went up first and he followed me, close behind.

– There's no point punishing Rosamaria, Frederico said: because it's all my fault. I've got to reform. Become far more efficient. Replace the alarm system, train the guards properly, get all my cataloguing up to date, check all the insurance policies. Probably I ought to go on a management course and learn how to do it. Oh dear. The one saving grace is that those cloths were indeed falling to pieces and probably past restoring.

He paused on a step halfway up. I paused too. His arms, gripping the sides of the ladder, encircled my hips. He began laughing into my back.

– Leonora told me something she discovered from her researches. There was an item in one of the convent account books, for washing. The nuns made menstrual cloths out of old altar linen that was falling to pieces, and the convent laundress washed everybody's rags once a month. It's rather fantastic, isn't it? Think of all those bleached white squares flapping on the clotheslines. That was their version of Rosamaria's patchwork banner I suppose.

– What if Rosamaria tells? I asked: won't you be in trouble?

Frederico was breathing hard behind me.

– She won't. She's already stipulated her bribe. I'm going to teach her how to use a video camera properly. All she managed to record on her trips to the Museum was a blue blur drifting about. She's going to shoot a short film on bears and bear bones. That will involve her going to the mountains for a few days with her parents. That should be safe enough. That should keep her out of trouble for a bit.

On the top of the giant slide we paused, panting.

– Let's go down together, Frederico proposed: much more fun.

He sat behind me on the toboggan-cushion. I sat between his legs. His arms embraced my waist. We pushed off over the edge and fell. How much I love that moment: no going back. We slipped over the lip down between the metal sides of the slide like sugar pouring from a jar then shot forwards, spiralling so fast I thought we would fly off into the air. It was like racing down a serpent's back. Whooo, Frederico sang behind me. At the bottom we dropped, laughing and winded, onto the rubber mat laid on the grass.

– Do you want to go back up? Frederico asked: do you want another go?

– No way, I said: once was quite enough. I want a cigarette.

We sat in the *caffe* on the edge of the funfair, smoking, drinking spritzers. Rosamaria buried her face in her candy-floss and then ate a carton of chips.

– I ought to ring Leonora, I said: find out how the

reconvened session has gone. Frederico, oughtn't you to have been there?

– Not on Sunday, he said: it's my day off.

– I want to show you the joke shop, Rosamaria said to me: it'll be closed, but you can see the window at any rate. Come on. Let's have a look.

We left behind the *caffe* and the funfair, the sparkling big wheel and the twinkling lights above shooting-ranges and tombola stalls, and walked towards the pedestrian crossing on the edge of the boulevard. Birds thronged the plane branches above our heads, chitter-chattering as they claimed their territory. The sky glowed blue, velvety soft, like the inside of one of Maude's jewel boxes.

Girls in silvered leather mini skirts and very high heels strolled the pavement against a backdrop of rushing cars. They didn't look Italian. Some looked eastern European. Under their makeup they seemed very young. Bunched and nervous, they shot us hostile glances as we went through the middle of their patch. We were rooks intruding on blackbirds, hopping onto their branch. Cruising up and down the boulevard flew the hawks. Go back home to your mothers, I wanted to cry to these lost girls: where is your home? But of course their mothers were very far away and some of them would never go home again.

– Glow-worms, Frederico said: for us, prostitutes and glow-worms, it's the same word.

A car slowed down, stopped. The driver surveyed the baby doll company parading past, wound his window down, lit a cigarette. A girl swayed across to the kerb, bent to talk to him, her pale skirt pulling up over her buttocks to display her G-string. I saw the driver's profile very clearly. Michael. He didn't notice me. Too occupied eyeing up the girl. She got into the front seat next to him and slammed the door. They accelerated off towards the station.

— Oh, Rosamaria cried: you can't see a thing. They've closed it up completely.

She pointed across the boulevard at a shuttered front in the stretch of shops on the far side.

— I expect that was by order of the Bishop, I said: no, perhaps just Sunday closing.

— Never mind, Frederico said: it's time to go home, anyway. Let's go. Let's take you home. Aurora, will you come and have supper?

— I'd love to. I'm hungry, I said: I missed lunch.

We dropped off Rosamaria at her parents' flat on the edge of town, then drove to Frederico's house. Without his mother there, and with no Giovanna calling from the kitchen, it didn't seem lonely so much as undomesticated, even wild, as though a certain set of rules had vanished, or dissolved. I stood in the back courtyard, pondering this, while Frederico put the car away. I felt relaxed in this peaceful place, listening to the crickets rasp in the grass, the house dog bark in the distance. I extended a hand and touched the warm stone of the wall. Above it the sky deepened to dusky blue.

– It's hard to explain, I said to Frederico when he emerged: something to do with Italian formality. I like it. One advances step by step towards friendship, towards intimacy, pausing whenever one needs to, for example moving from *lei* to *tu*. Then suddenly one's inside a friendship, not outside.

– You only find it hard to explain because you're not used to putting your feelings into words, Frederico said: now me, I've had years of practice. For example, I haven't yet told you about my dream last night. I was a bear hibernating in the woods and Rosamaria was a hunter, one of those Amazons, trying to pull my bones out of my fur. I shouted at her: I don't want to be a relic! Then the dawn light came up and chased her away.

– So in fact, I said: you had guessed at the truth even before she confessed.

– Masculine intuition, Frederico said.

He unlocked and pushed open the kitchen door.

– Now, let's find some wine. Then we'll have a stroll.

Glass in hand, he showed me, as blueness gathered, the parts of the grounds I had not seen on my previous visit: the *brolo* with its rows of tall vines, and the *grande prato*, a big meadow edged by poplars, leading to a fenced wood rustling with shadows.

– Too dark soon to go for a proper walk in the wood tonight, Frederico said: I'll take you another time. Now let's eat. All right with you if we eat outside?

He cooked and I sat at the kitchen table, watching. He

carried the supper out on a tray. I followed him, a bottle of wine under each arm. We sat in the darkest part of the garden, the indigo shade under one of the huge cedars at the side of the house. A silvery trace of moon emerged from behind a profile of gutter, glimmered white on the top of the wall. Inside this container of stone we were held in a second box, enclosed by sweetsmelling, gathering night. While we ate and talked, the sky thickened with stars. Our circular stone table held a single candle, the wine, a bowl of pasta, a plate of prosciutto, a bowl of salad, a bowl of peaches.

Whisking my bottle of citronella out of my handbag, I anointed myself, before eating, against the circling mosquitoes. Offered the bottle, Frederico waved it away.

– Don't they bite you? I asked.

– They don't like my aftershave, he said: too spicy for them. They don't come near me.

The pasta, dressed with anchovies, parsley, garlic and white wine, was delicious. I sat back, sighing with pleasure.

– So. Was everything all right with the police? I didn't like to ask you in front of Rosamaria.

– Not as bad as I thought, Frederico said: they are indeed going to close the Museum for a couple of days but not ask me to cancel the show completely. So we'll open late, that's all. It could have been much worse.

We finished the rest of the food, and the wine. We sat quietly in the fragrant darkness.

– Stay the night if you'd like to, Frederico said: we've got plenty of room. Then I can drive you back into town in the morning, if that's what you would like.

The tip of his cigarette glowed red as though he too were a glow-worm.

– It is getting late, I agreed: thank you. That's a good idea.

– Let me just put these things in the kitchen, Frederico said: and I'll show you the guestroom.

I followed him to the second storey.

– This was formerly where the nuns slept, Frederico explained: now my mother has that room at the end, and I have this one at the other end, and in between we keep rooms for the family when they visit, and then the guests stay up here.

I followed him through a curtained doorway and up a spiral of stone, a coil of air mounting inside the little tower you could see from the garden. At the top of this was a small square room. Frederico's fingers hovered just above the light switch. Through the dimness I made out windows on four sides, a wide bed in the middle, heaped invitingly with fat white pillows. An open stone staircase, narrow and steep, rose in one corner.

– Just above you is the loggia, Frederico said: good for midnight star-gazing. I used to sleep up there sometimes when I was a boy. I called it the tower of the four winds.

Frederico seemed oddly nervous. He fiddled with the pillows on the bed, straightening them, and carried on chattering.

– I think you are better off sleeping here. In the loggia the light does wake you very early in the morning because there are no walls, just four columns, no windows or blinds. It's all open to the sky under the roof. I'll show you tomorrow if you like.

– This is a very nice room, I said: I'm sure I shall sleep well in it.

– You see there are lamps all around, Frederico said: let's switch on this corner one, then the light won't be too bright.

I sat down experimentally on the bed. Just right: not too hard and not too soft.

Frederico seemed in no hurry to leave. He sat down next to me. He surprised me by taking my hand in both of his, squeezing it, then stroking it, and gazing into my eyes.

– Aurora, he said: there is something I want to tell you. May I tell you what it is?

I smiled at him. At last, I thought, he is making me his confidante. At last he trusts me enough to unburden himself to me and come out to me.

Into my voice I threw all the tenderness I could muster. Not wanting to alarm him in any way or disrupt the confidential mood, I spoke in a whisper.

– Frederico, of course you may. I'm delighted you want to tell me. I'm really touched.

Frederico caressed my hand. He blushed. His shyness touched me. I did a rapid search of novels in my head, seeking for some reassuring words. Of course. *Villette*. The scene where Lucy encourages Paulina to open her heart and pour out her feelings of love for Dr Bretton.

– How calm and secluded it feels here, I said, quoting Lucy as accurately as I could: how peaceful.

– Aurora, Frederico said: you know I like you very much, don't you?

Bitterness suddenly rose up and overwhelmed me.

– You like me because I'm Cecil's widow, I said: you told me so, more or less. Everyone only likes me because I'm Tom's widow, or Cecil's, or Hugh's.

– Oh Aurora, Frederico said: perhaps you should stop getting married so often, then. Give yourself a chance.

He put an arm around my shoulders. He lifted his free hand and swept it down the side of my face. The gesture startled me. It seemed almost flirtatious.

– Aurora, you don't have to treat me like a mosquito and swat me away. I won't bite you. I just want to be near you. Do you really find me so repellent?

I removed his arm. All this beating around the bush exasperated me. Were gay men always this complicated?

– You don't have to do that, I said: it's not necessary. Please don't be embarrassed, Frederico. I know what you are trying to tell me. I'm very broadminded. Really I am. I do understand.

– No, you don't, Frederico said: not at all. I am in complete despair.

He stood up. He began to unbuckle his belt.

– Frederico, what are you doing? I cried.

— I want to show you how much I like you, Frederico said: you don't believe in words so deeds will have to do.

His perfectly cut jeans concertinaed around his ankles. His boxer shorts followed. He stood and faced me. I gazed at his erect cock. He began to unbutton his shirt.

— But Frederico, I stammered: you don't like women. Not to go to bed with, anyway.

Frederico removed the rest of his clothes in a trice, and leaped back gracefully into bed. He took me in his arms. They were surprisingly strong. They wrapped themselves lightly around me and held me.

— I'm too fat for anyone to fancy me, I moaned: and I'm so old.

— You're not fat at all, Frederico said: you're just right. And you're not old. You're eternally young. You're a goddess, with the body of a goddess.

— It must be all those lunches I've missed, I said: I thought I was fat.

Frederico kissed me. His tongue, soft and wide, filled my mouth. Irresistible. I kissed him back. Then we stopped, took a breather, kissed each other's necks.

— As long as you love your mother, he whispered into my ear: it's all right. Fat women, thin women, you can love them all. *Embarras de richesses.* You are my ideal. You are amazingly beautiful and sexy, Aurora. Surely you know that.

He began caressing my breasts through my dress. Then he undid all my buttons, tugged down my shoulder straps, unfastened my bra. He pulled off my knickers, slid his fingers in, found my clitoris, circled it. Very gently, round and round, then more firmly. I couldn't stop myself. My hips thrust towards him. I swelled up, fat as the pillows on the bed. I grasped his cock in my hand and guided him inside me. Cock and fingers and cunt all mixed together.

– I thought you only cared about art history, I babbled: and trousers and museums.

– Don't be silly, Aurora, Frederico shouted.

Now I knew he was a man like any other. I yielded and gave myself up to the moment. Perhaps, indeed, I was rather like Lucy in *Villette*, who in Thackeray's view turned her attention too rapidly from one man to another, but, hell, what did novelists know about anything?

Chapter Seven

– Soon be there, Aurora.

Sister Clara's driving left no doubt about that. We sped along the *autostrada* towards Venice airport, in the yellow convent minibus, at a hundred and forty kilometres an hour. I sat stiff and sweating and upright in the passenger seat, unused to wearing a head-dress, to such a bulk of wool around my neck and knees. Leonora had lent me an outfit nicely judged to occupy halfway territory between old-fashioned pretty and modern ugly: black veil over white coif, three-quarters-length black dress, black rain-coat, black stockings and shoes.

– They'll be looking for a curvy blonde in red silk, she pointed out: you've got a much better chance of getting away if you flee dressed as a nun.

On my knee reposed a nunly black felt reticule con-taining my false passport and air ticket. I had abandoned the gold canister to a waste bin near the Museum, together with most of its contents. I didn't need them now. Once I'd wiped the pistol free of fingerprints and thrown it out into the empty air from the topmost step under the arcade leading up to the convent, I felt relieved. Different. Changes, of all sorts, as I had begun to suspect even before my departure, had indeed come upon me. With no pistol to wrap, my box of sanitary towels was superfluous. The menopause was the true miracle after all, I realised: the squares of bleached cloth remaining marvellously white. Poor St Elizabeth, falling pregnant with John the Baptist just when she thought she was safe, dutifully embracing the pregnant Virgin and listening to her sing *Magnificat*. Whereas my song of praise was not for God, not for a baby, but for sex with Frederico. How light and buoyant that made me feel. Every time I thought of him I felt a grin spread over my face. Can a cunt smile? That's where the grin started.

I shut my eyes as Sister Clara put her foot down, hooted, and pulled out to pass a vast lorry. She felt me flinch, and laughed.

– Learn to drive, dear Aurora, and then you won't be scared.

– It's my next project, I promised her: I'm going to check out my Italian ancestors when I return, and find my Italian family, and for that I shall need to be able to drive.

We crept past the lorry. The nuns at my convent school taught us to compose ourselves for sleep by contemplating the possibility of dying in the night. Arms crossed on our breasts, we were to meditate on the Four Last Things: death, judgment, hell and heaven. With death by juggernaut imminent on the *autostrada* I found myself unable to think forwards. Instead, going backwards, I began to reflect on the formative events, the Four Blasted Things, of my adolescence.

Mama died when I was twelve. Papa couldn't cope. Maude stepped in. I got into big trouble.

On Mama's death, my mind necessarily became much occupied with questions of salvation. I dared tell no one how much I worried whether my mother had got safely to heaven. She couldn't be in hell, not my sweet Mama who sang to me in bed at night, taught me how to plait my hair and make sponge cakes, let me try on her high-heeled shoes. But perhaps she languished in purifying purgatorial fires, whence I ought to rescue her. If I didn't offer her a helping hand she might be stuck down there for centuries.

Simple protocol. The nuns taught me what to do. Their ideal of grieving commanded you pray as often and as much as you could, got up early to go to Mass every morning, made sacrifices, offered up all forms of self-deprivation and self-oppression possible, each extra penance undertaken cheerfully for the sake of that Holy Soul. You made novenas, which gained you extra points; you intoned certain invocations blessed by the Pope and carrying Indulgences. These were special graces, counted in days of torment avoided and written off; so many days off purgatory. Once you were dead, you presented them, like savings certificates cancelling your debts, at the turnstile: look, guv, I'm only staying a thousand years down here, after all, not two thousand. In the economy of expiation, piled-up prayers earned a form of interest. This, meant for your own spiritual savings account, could be switched to someone else's, spent on their benefit, when you instructed your heavenly banker to effect the transfer. Offer it up for the Holy Souls, the nuns exhorted us whenever anything unpleasant happened, and so we did.

I had explained all this to Leonora earlier in the day, when I ran up to the convent to say goodbye to her.

– I know all that, Leonora said: things were just as bad in Italy, *cara*. You don't have to remind me.

– Yes, but I've got to tell you this in my own way, I said: OK? We extroverts, when we do get round to examining our feelings, we go to town. This may take some time.

We were sitting in the confessional in the convent library. Leonora's updated version of this ecclesiastical staple placed two wooden beach huts, one yellow and one blue, closely side by side, facing forwards like two old friends looking out together at the sea, but in this case at tall shelves of books. The serried volumes swept forwards like waves.

The beach huts stood an inch apart. Leonora had had little windows cut into their adjacent walls so that the inhabitants could converse easily hut to hut. Inside each one, the furnishings comprised a striped green and white deckchair, a wooden shelf, and an empty crate, upended, on which you could perch your book, or your cup of coffee, or your glass of wine. I sat in the yellow hut and

Leonora in the blue. The huts had seemingly just flown in, like the Virgin's little house at Nazareth magically transported on angels' wings to Loreto.

— I'm listening, Leonora said: go on.

I should have asked for a sign that Mama had reached her heavenly destination. Not that I'd necessarily have expected a vision of the Madonna or similar. Everybody knew that the Virgin never travelled to misty grey English suburbs like Greenhill. She preferred hot places, like the south of France, or Portugal, or indeed Italy. Nor could I wish for a burning bush suddenly to bloom outside the flat's window, or a couple of cherubim to float past giving the thumbs up. But perhaps I could have seen Mama in a dream. I didn't. My dreams featured only strangers, all undergoing torture. To ward them off I redoubled my efforts. To show God I was serious about getting Mama out of the Satanic kitchen, equipped with grilles over pits of red coals, where sous-chef devils prodded her with pitchforks as they turned her over and basted her, I widened my attention to take note of other suffering souls, in particular those of the little black babies we heard so much about at school.

Infants who died unbaptised, innocent because of their extreme youth, hence their incapacity for sin, were sent to Limbo, a specially designed crêche, not as unpleasant as Purgatory but still lacking the amenities of Heaven. Here they would have to wait until the end of the world when Jesus would harrow Hell, open Purgatory, unlock the babies' prison and lead everybody, in one great Sunday School outing, up to glory. He carried a red-crossed banner, according to the holy picture on the classroom wall, so that nobody would lose Him in the crowds. He looked rather like the harassed tour guides in Venice or Florence or Rome, with their beribboned umbrellas raised aloft, waving the tourists forward into yet another cathedral or museum. The Church's point was that saving souls was personally up to you: get the black babies baptised and they were spared Limbo, should they suddenly perish, and could hop straight on the Up escalator towards their Heavenly Father.

Baptisms cost money. Threepence per step up the heavenly ladder. Two shillings and sixpence in total per baby. My pocket money, hoarded each week, did not stretch to more than a baptism per month. That was not enough. I had to raise more cash.

– How did you do that? Leonora asked.

– I charged for sex, I replied.

I stole the idea from *The Passionflower Hotel*, a novel which the nuns would not have wished us to read, and which circulated, amid gasps and giggles, behind raised desk-lids, from classroom to classroom, its lurid cover disguised by a brown paper wrapper.

This story of a schoolgirls' brothel I re-enacted at Girl Guide camp the summer I turned thirteen and discovered that a troop of Boy Scouts was camping in the neighbouring field.

We of the Swallow, Thrush, Peewit and Chaffinch patrols had eaten our fried mince and boiled spuds, lowered the Union Jack from the flagpole, sung our sunset anthem, been shooed into our ridge tents. Here, in those pre-sleeping-bag days, we slept in rolls of blankets secured by big steel safety pins. Damp canvas smelled of damp grass. I peered out through the flap. Starlit darkness. Captain and Kim huddled, two rounded silhouettes, by the dying fire. They took a last mug of cocoa together at this time.

They had taught us tracking as an essential woodland skill. Barefoot, my makeup bag nipped between my teeth, I crept past them through the shadows wrapping the chemical lavs, into the hedge that formed the boundary between our camp and that of the Scouts. The Scout I had liaised with earlier directed towards me a flow of clients. I charged according to what they looked at, and what they touched. A nipple. A whole breast. A flash of pubic hair.

Too much rustling and smothered laughter brought discovery. Captain and Kim hollered distress calls, frogmarched me off, put me in a tent in solitary confinement for the rest of the night. The next morning, Maude having been sent for and standing at attention with us in our solemn horseshoe, our leaders gave us a parade-ground address on chastity. Then Captain formally expelled me from the Girl Guides and commanded me to leave camp before I corrupt anyone else. Those poor wee Scouts. I, a

Child of Mary, had betrayed my vows and caused fresh agony to the suffering Virgin at the foot of the Cross. Probably to Mama as well. Everybody got on with their square-lashing. I had made ten shillings in half an hour, which wasn't bad.

– I swore to myself, I said: that the next time I committed a crime I would get away with it and escape being found out.

– And did you? Leonora asked.

– More or less, I said: until recently, anyway.

With Frederico there had been one tense moment, in the middle of the night, in between bouts of graceful, vigorous, joyful sex.

– No, my darling Aurora, no. Just because we have made love we do not have to get married. I am not going to propose marriage to you. I cannot help noticing, from what you yourself have told me, that all three of your husbands have died mysterious, not to say violent, deaths. I think we should simply remain lovers and good friends.

– Edmund wasn't quite as lucky as you, then, Leonora said.

– I think he was probably relieved, I said: he knew he'd gone a bit too far. I think he was grateful to me, really, for taking his bag from him the way I did.

He hadn't been able to argue. They were late for their plane and had to rush. Arrived back in Padenza, taking the suitcase to my room at the Museum, I had been unable to resist picking the lock and examining the contents.

How clever of Edmund to wear the antique dresses he stole, and make his escape from the Museum disguised as a ghost. How stupid of me not to have recognised him and Maude dancing, both in drag, at the *festa*. But my mind had been on other things at the time, such as Michael holding me in his arms. Sexual desire can be a terrible clouder of judgement, a terrible blurrer of vision. Hadn't I found that out several times already in my life?

– Anyway, I said: now that he and Maude have decided to get married they sound very happy. They told me on the phone this morning that they plan to do a double act at one of the drag cabaret clubs in the East End. Maude hopes they'll win the *Grande Dame* competition and get onto TV.

– Maude is a magnificent woman, Leonora said.

– Yes, I agreed: and she is a magnificent man, too.

I hesitated.

– Perhaps there's something else I should tell you.

– Go on, *cara*. But make it quick. The bell for lunch will be ringing soon. And in any case, since you've suddenly decided to change your plans and catch the early afternoon plane, you'll have to be off any minute as well.

– I bumped into Michael earlier, I said.

– So?

– I don't quite know how to put this, I said.

I like a good thriller as much as anyone, but I could never write one because I am hopeless at plotting. I could never be a conspirator, either. Too complicated. I am not an accomplished criminal. In fact I do not consider myself a criminal at all, simply an ordinary person caught up in dramas beyond her control, who just reacts to events as they occur and does her best at any given moment. I'm not even really much good at lying. I can do poker-face for smuggling drugs, but making up elaborate stories is beyond me. I did wonder, now, whether I had found a happy ending. Frederico was so funny, affectionate, and clever, such a skilled cook, and so good in bed. He seemed the perfect man.

A warning bell clanged in my memory. Hastily I promised myself that this time I would be careful, at the beginning, not to become too romantic, so that I would not feel forced to compensate, later on, by experiencing too much disappointment.

On the other hand, Frederico's background was undeniably far posher than mine. Were we too different? Could the relationship last? I hadn't a clue.

That morning, I'd woken feeling extremely cheerful. Frederico woke up at the same time. We made sleepy love. He entered me from behind, one hand reaching around me to touch my clitoris at the same time. We came, went on lying there wrapped together, eased ourselves out of bed, showered. Frederico rushed me downstairs into the gloomy dining-room for a cup of espresso, a slice of almond cake. Then he pulled me down onto the carpet and made love to me again.

– I've always wanted to do that here. Eating always makes me think about sex. That and books.

Clothes tangled around our feet, tongues tasting of coffee and sugar. We came in each other's mouths. Then he drove me into town. Blue mist hid the horizon and hung like steam above the fields of maize. The sun was a golden shimmer behind cloud.

– What did you dream about last night? I asked.

– Can't remember. Put some music on, dear Aurora, why don't you?

I scrabbled among the CDs littering the shelf to the right of the dashboard.

– Bob Dylan all right?

Blood on the Tracks boomed from the car stereo. We both sang along to 'Tangled Up In Blue'. We swooped across the river.

Frederico dropped me outside the Museum. His hands still on the wheel, he turned to me and kissed me.

– Shall we meet for lunch? And then later, if you like, I could come to see you off at the airport.

– I'd like that, I said.

– Oh Aurora, he said: you'll come back soon, won't you?

– I will, I promised: I've got so much research for the deli still to do.

He headed off into the carpark. I wandered into the Piazza, towards the Caffe Elizabetta, in search of more coffee.

Right in the middle of that sunswept place swirling with tourists and shoppers, Michael barred my path. He was wearing a black linen Armani suit over a white T-shirt. He looked bronzed, and muscled, and ready for anything. His socks were invisible.

– Is that a gun in your pocket? I asked him: or are you just pleased to see me?

– This is yours, isn't it, Aurora?

He held out my pistol. I took it from him and inspected it.

– I do believe it is, I said: thank you so much. I'd hate to have lost it. You know it belonged to my mother. It's a precious heirloom.

– I confiscated the bullets from Leonora and re-loaded it, he said: in order to test that it works. I can't really believe you know how to fire it. You're just pretending, aren't you?

– No, I said.

He watched my face. I hesitated. He scowled.

– Come on, Aurora. Time to give yourself up. Confess. You killed all three of your husbands, one after the other, didn't you? We've had our suspicions of you for a long time. It took a while to work out that it was the same woman, i.e., you in all three cases, but finally we got there.

Most criminals use aliases. I had just kept getting married and changing my name.

– We've got all the evidence we need, Michael said.

Damn. I could have sworn I'd covered my traces most efficiently.

– What evidence? I asked: mainly circumstantial, surely?

– Hugh left a letter with Father Kenneth, to be forwarded to the police in the event of his unexpected death. Father Kenneth found it yesterday, on his return to the presbytery, and realised he'd forgotten to post it. He opened it and read it and rang me immediately.

I sighed.

– He wasn't a VAT inspector for nothing, your husband, Michael said: he knew the importance of keeping accurate records. He had put two and two together and worked out, from what you had told him yourself, that you had been in the vicinity when Cecil fell out of the window, and when Tom fell off the balcony, and that you were the only person with a motive for killing either of them. Father Kenneth couldn't help remembering what Maude and Edmund had told him, that you were the only person with Hugh when he fell off the cliff at Lands End.

– Marriage is awfully difficult, Michael, I murmured: adapting oneself to another person is not easy.

Michael ignored my plea for sympathy. He narrowed his slate-blue eyes.

– What a stroke of luck we were both bound for Italy, wasn't it?

– Not synchronicity after all? I asked.

– Don't be silly, Aurora. We'd re-opened our investigation into Cecil's death before Hugh died. I planned my trip to Italy in the hopes of gathering information we'd missed first time round. Once I realised you were on your way as well, I was sure that sooner or later I'd catch you committing a crime. I nearly got you for drugs, and for conspiracy to murder a Bishop.

Not to mention protecting the identity of a thief or two, I thought.

– I don't think much of your powers of deduction, I said: all you've had to do is listen to stories other people tell you. And it's taken you a long time even to get round to doing that.

– And now, Michael continued: the moment has arrived to arrest you. I must ask you to accompany me to the police station immediately. If you don't come freely you're in even worse trouble. While as for that nancy-boy you flap your eyelashes at, he's in big danger of losing his job on the grounds of aiding and abetting a murderer.

My happiness with Frederico, and his with me, was under threat. All my hopes of making a fresh start, of putting the past behind me, suddenly seemed fragile.

To be stopped at this juncture felt deeply unfair.

I hope it is clear by now that I cannot cope with anger, cannot tolerate frustration, don't know how to negotiate conflict. That's to say, I'm not good at relationships with men who try to thwart my desires.

Also, being an extrovert, as Michael himself had pointed out, I tend to act first and reflect afterwards.

What else could I do?

This was an emergency. Mama would have been proud of my sang-froid. I raised my pistol. I aimed it.

– No, Michael said.

– Yes, I said.

I fired.

Reader, I murdered him.